A Most
Remarkable
Life

The Collected Works of
Robert Huddleston
WWII COMBAT PILOT & FEDERAL OFFICIAL

Volume II: Plays & Sketches

A Most Remarkable Life: The Collected Works of Bob Huddleston, Volume 2

Copyright © Robert Huddleston 2024
All rights reserved.

ISBN: 979-8-218-41219-7

Fiction/Nonfiction/Historical/General

Book design by Kelly Prelipp Lojk.

Back cover author's photo by John Haynes.

Published by Robert Huddleston
Chapel Hill, North Carolina
hobartjr1924@gmail.com

Dedicated to the dear friends and volunteer actors
at Carolina Meadows that helped me bring
my stage plays to life.

The Collected Works
of Robert Huddleston

Volume II ◈ Plays & Sketches
(some of them true)

The Legacy of Hiroshima *(poem)* . . . . *vii*

◈ ◈ ◈

Robert & Ava: The Bard & the Beauty *(play)* . . *1*

Ava, Robert, & Friends *(essay)* 29

Exploitation: Dawn of the Cold War *(play)* . 35

Uncle Edgar's Secret List *(play)* 97

**I'll Get the Check: A (Probably True)
Political Fable in One Act** *(play)* 115

The Resurrection of Louise Brooks *(play)* . . *157*

**The Long Snooze: A 25th Anniversary
Fantasy** *(play)* *183*

◈ ◈ ◈

About the Author 205

The Legacy
of Hiroshima

Bomb, bomb, and the war will end
This the message our leaders send
Tens and hundreds bombers went
To kill, to maim, to destroy and rent
A civilized world having lost its way
It proved impossible to gain a stay
Carpet bombing occured yesterday
Is one bomb per city a better way?

– a World War II fighter pilot

Robert & Ava

'The Bard & the Beauty'

An original one-act play
*An intimate conversation
between the poet Robert Graves
and the actress Ava Gardner*

The play is set in the living room of Graves's home in Deya on the island of Majorca, Spain. The time is 1955. The room is modestly furnished with two comfortable wing chairs, a small side table with brandy and two glasses, several books, and a bookcase with assorted books.

THE CHARACTERS
(in order of appearance)

Robert Graves: English poet and novelist in his mid-sixties.

Beryl Graves: Wife of Robert Graves, younger than her husband.

Ava Gardner: Famous movie actress in her early thirties.

THE PLAY

(Robert Graves enters carrying a book from the table and is headed to one of the chairs when he pauses and addresses the audience.)

Robert: I don't believe we've met. I am Robert Graves, a poet ... an English poet. (*Pauses and smiles*) I must confess, I am eagerly awaiting a visit by the beautiful American actress Ava Gardner. Mutual friends in Madrid arranged the visit. Miss Gardner, so they informed me, has developed an interest in poetry. (*Smiles*) She is, of course, coming to the proper place. It is why I have settled here in the village of Deya on the Spanish island of Majorca. (*Begins to read, then turns back to address the audience with a smile*). This might well become an interesting discourse ...

perhaps, even an intimate one! You may listen, but you must hold what you hear in confidence.

(*Robert proceeds to read. In a few moments Beryl and Ava enter.*)

Beryl: Robert, may I present our beautiful guest ... ? (*Graves starts to rise*)

Ava: Please ... relax. (*She leans over and kisses him on the cheek.*)

Beryl: Ava, I know you will enjoy your conversation with Robert ...

Ava: I know I will ...

Beryl: But I warn you, he can be quite impish at times.

Ava: (*Laughing*) That I can match ... I've learned to deal with imps ... large, masculine imps.

Beryl: Then I'll leave the two of you to return when lunch is ready ...

Ava: Beryl, thank you very much for your kind reception.

Beryl: 'Til lunch

Robert: Thank you, Beryl.

(*Beryl leaves and Ava sit in the second chair.*)

Robert: Well, Miss Gardner, might I first ask about your need for a walking aid?

Ava: Please, make that Ava. You may. I turned my ankle seeking to escape a pack of paparazzi attempting to photograph me at my worst. It's OK now. (*Smiles*) I'll leave the cane for a memento.

Robert: It will be cherished ... Ava .... As you prefer ... I was about to welcome you to Deya.

Ava: Thanks for the invitation. Might I call you Robert?

Robert: If we were strangers, it would be Graves ... or in England, Captain Graves. As friends, it shall be Robert.

Ava: "Robert." I like that.

Robert: (*Smiling*) Now, if we were to become lovers, we must have pet names. But, of course, this is quite unlikely ... even impossible. Does this disappoint you?

Ava: (*Pauses, not quite certain as to how to respond.*) Well, Robert, I know we shall be very good friends ...

Robert: Yes, Ava, very good friends.

Ava: (*Laughing*) Now that our relationship is settled, I owe you an apology.

Robert: (*Smiling*) And what is it you need to apologize for?

Ava: For avoiding you when we first met at the home of our mutual friends, Ricardo and Betty Sicre ...

Robert: I did notice that ...

Ava: I asked someone who you were and was told you were a British scientist.

Robert: (*Smiling*) On that basis, you were fully justified.

Ava: Thank you!

Robert: And the Graveses thank you for the huge bouquet of red roses you sent ...

Ava: My way of saying how pleased I was to receive your invitation.

Robert: Now, let me reciprocate with a touch of Spanish brandy. It will cause us to relax.

(*Brandy with two glasses is on a side table.*)

Ava: Ooooh. I'd like that ...

Robert: (*Pours two glasses from a decanter as he talks.*) Fair warning, it is rather fiery.

Ava: (*As he serves her*) I can handle it ... (*She takes the glass and looks around the room.*) This is a wonderful place. Deya ... your beautiful house and garden. (*She moves to the bookcase.*) This room ... (*She sips the brandy then sets the glass on the table and takes a book from the shelf.*) Poems by Robert

Graves. (*She puts it back and takes another.*) *Poems, 1926-1930* by Robert Graves. (*She returns it and takes another.*) *Collected Poems* by Robert Graves. (*She returns the book.*) Tell me, Robert, (*smiling*) are there no other poets that interest you?

Robert: (*Smiles*) Very few ... very few truly good poets ... Look on the second shelf, far right.

Ava: (*Takes the book as directed and reads.*) *Collected Poems* by Robert Frost ...

Robert: Yes ... and the other American poet I recommend is cummings ...

Ava: Cummings?

Robert: e.e. cummings. He prefers no capital letters. Both Frost and cummings are quite good. I'll see that you have copies.

Ava: Help me, Robert, why is poetry important? I asked Hemingway and all he offered was "ask Graves." OK ... I'm asking ...

Robert: (*Smiling*) Well, young lady, if you enjoy words, a truly fine poem can make words sing. But, even more importantly, poetry can help one to understand themselves.

Ava: How?

Robert: That, I will not answer. If you pursue poetry, the answer will become quite clear.

Ava: (*Returns the book to the shelf and sits.*) All right. Tell me, Robert, what brought you here, to this rather isolated village?

Robert: I came here in 1929, with an American poet ... a wonderful poet. We built this stone house that we called *Ca N'Alluny*. Poetry is emotion expressed in a fertile environment, and this village meets that need. So, we created a small artistic community. Then, in 1936, the Civil War forced us to leave Majorca. My relationship to this American poet ended, and I met and married the lovely Beryl.

Ava: Where? Where did the two of you meet?

Robert: We met in London in 1937. She was a recent Oxford graduate.

Ava: Younger?

Robert: (*Smiling*) Much younger. We came here in 1946 with three of our children, William, Lucia, and Juan. Our youngest, Tomas, was born here. This is our home and this is where I will die ...

Ava: Not soon, I hope ...

Robert: *Tempus edax rerum* ... Time devours everything. Now, back to you ... your interest in visiting here ... with me. Why?

Ava: My interest in poetry. I met Ernest Hemingway recently when I was in the hospital suffering from a kidney stone. (*Laughs*) And he asked if he could have the stone ...

Robert: That is a rather unusual item to collect ...

Ava: Just talk ... his idea of humor. But when I mentioned my interest in poetry, he was serious. Said Spain was the place and Robert Graves unrivaled as a poet. The name took me back to the Sicres and Betty took it from there.

Robert: Yes, she said you needed to get away from Madrid ... had an interest in poetry and ... not surprising ... I was eager to offer an invitation ...

Ava: And I to receive it ...

Robert: Speaking of Hemingway, we have met, but I found him rather aloof. Later, I was reminded that my very good American friend Tom Mathews—we had met as undergraduates at Oxford—had married Hemingway's ex-wife, Martha Gellhorn. Apparently they did not part on pleasant terms. As a contemporary, however, we have much in common: the war, injuries, difficulties with women (*Smiles*). As writers, no! He is the novelist. I am a poet.

Ava: A great poet, so they say ... But you are also a novelist; *I, Claudius* is often mentioned.

Robert: Writing novels is the means of support while writing poetry. I fell in love with poetry at the tender age of fifteen, and it has been my life. But, before we discuss poetry, I need to know more about you, other than the obvious: that you are a very beautiful actress. Why are you in Spain? But wait, would you mind coming around and massaging my upper back?

Ava: It will be a pleasure. (*She move behind his chair and begins massaging.*)

Robert: Ah! Wonderful. I must avoid sitting too long. Please continue.

Ava: Why I came to Spain? Work and marriage. I needed to get away. I'm divorcing my husband ...

Robert: The singer ...

Ava: The famous Voice ... the great Frank Sinatra. There is another reason. A new movie set in Spain is being discussed, and I am being considered for a part. This is one reason I have rented a place in Madrid.

Robert: The movie is ...?

Ava: First, allow me to offer you a small gift. (*She moves to her chair and takes a book out of her bag.*) May I present you with *Fiesta*, the English printing of *The Sun Also Rises*, signed by Hemingway? It was discovered in a London bookstore ... (*She hands him the book.*)

Robert: (*Opens the book*) Published in London in 1927. I suppose the American publisher came up with "The Sun Also Rises." Beryl has read the book, and we have discussed the plot. This is the basis for a possible film?

Ava: It is ...

Robert: (*With a mischievous grin*) And you will play the very beautiful Lady Brett Ashley?

Ava: I will. And your description is most appreciated ...

Robert: And well deserved. I am not one for cinemas, but I will look forward to *Fiesta*, or whatever they choose to title it ...

Ava: I took the script to Hemingway, who was in El Escorial, and he hit the ceiling, yelling how they had debased and distorted his story ...

Robert: (*Scowling*) How? ...

Ava: The casting ... Tyrone Power to play the leading man, Jake Barnes. And one of your countrymen, Errol Flynn, would play a key role as the Scotsman Mike Campbell.

Robert: (*With a slight sneer*) Not exactly one of my countrymen. Flynn is an Australian.

Ava: (*Smiling*) I thought you shared the same queen?

Robert: (*Smiling*) We do indeed ... with many primitives.

Ava: Shame on you, Robert. Errol and I were never lovers, but we dated when I first came to Hollywood. He was fun, gallant, and a well-mannered man with a great sense of humor. Yes, later on he drank too much and was involved in many scandals. But the Errol Flynn I knew had style, Robert. Real style ...

Robert: May I stand corrected?

Ava: You may.

Robert: Back to Hemingway's objections...

Ava: In addition to Tyrone and Errol, the cast would include Eddie Albert as Jake's pal, Bill Gorton, and Mel Ferrer as Robert Cohn, all in their forties. Hemingway's characters were disillusioned young men in their twenties, just out of that terrible war, and these guys are too old even be drafted. Papa did say that he guessed I would do as Lady Brett ...

Robert: (*Beaming*) And I agree. Am I correct, Lady Ashley is—how did Hemingway express it?—sexually uninhibited?

Ava: (*Laughing*) Robert, it is a role I relish.

Robert: And (*Smirking*) fond of bullfighters?

Ava: (*Smiling*) I've been there.

Robert: I know. I confess to seeing *Pandora* ...

Ava: ... *and the Flying Dutchman*

Robert:... with a bullfighter

Ava: (*Smiles*) With a bullfighter.

Robert: The film generated much attention in the Spanish press.

Ava: How well I know. My co-star, Mario Cabré, announced to the press that he was in love with me. It drove Frank up the wall, and he came to Spain and demanded I never see the guy . I had to explain Mario was my co-star and I had to see him. Hubby retreated ... and I saw a divorce in our future. No one possesses me, married or otherwise.

Robert: Let's talk about how you ... How did you get into acting?

Ava: Rags to riches story. Poor kid from the backwoods of North Carolina. A photograph taken by my sister's husband drew the interest of Hollywood. Too young to understand what I was getting into.

Robert: When were you born?

Ava: 1922. Went to Hollywood at nineteen. Two very short, bad marriages. My marriages were all bad ... no more!

Robert: When were you first married?

Ava: Not long after I had arrived in Hollywood. To Mickey Rooney. Too soon. Much too young. (*Smiles*) But too old to be a virgin ...

Robert: (*Smiles*) Something I can relate to.

Ava: You're kidding! (*Robert responds with a smile.*) If not, you're the first man I've known who admitted to having ever been virginal. (*Smiles*) Maybe I can find one here in Spain ...

Robert: (*Smiling*) Back to your forsaking marriage. My second marriage has been wonderful ... Beryl and four children ... three with us now. Were you ever in love?

Ava: Yes, I was ... not always ... in love with Frank ... a love/hate relationship. God, how we did fight. Fuck—sorry—and fight. Hellava way to live. No more!

Robert: But, being in love never deterred you from giving in to lust?

Ava: Love, I've learned the hard way, can be a real pain. Lust I enjoy and forget.

Robert: (*Frowning*) Lust is giving away something that belongs to someone else ...

Ava: ... to the someone you love?

Robert: Exactly. The act of love belongs to two people, in the way secrets are shared. You Americans, it seems, have your focus on sex and trivialize love. As a result, there is far less interest in poetry than in England.

Ava: What has you believing this?

Robert: Your entertainment, especially the cinema and television. Also, your many divorces ...

Ava: Robert, would you mind if I work on this? (*Smiling*) Shifting from lust to love may not be easy ...

Robert: (*Smiling*) And it could be I've come too late to influence your behavior ...

Ava: (*Smiling*) I suspect, much too late ...

Robert: (*With a sly smile*) Might I ask you how compatible you were with your three husbands?

Ava: (*Smiling*) You might. But if I translate "compatible" from English to American, I gather you're asking how each was in bed. Right?

Robert: (*Smiling*) My good lady, you may translate as you wish.

Ava: (*With a wide grin and raising her voice*) Darn good! (*Lowers her voice and speaks in a conspiratorial tone.*) Each different, but each, in their own way, damn good ... But I've known better!

Robert: Um ... (*Not used to such an outspoken lady*) ... When did you first appear in a film?

Ava: That would be ... (*Pause*) 1942.

Robert: And your latest?

Ava: That would be last year. *The Barefoot Contessa* with Humphrey Bogart

Robert: (*Acting the imp!*) Now, if you don't mind my asking ... When, in your opinion, were you at your best—not regarding your acting, but your appearance?

Ava: Robert, that's a dead giveaway of where your interests lie.

Robert: (*Smiling*) My dear, when you come to understand poetry, you'll understand the point of this.

Ava: OK, Robert. Not long ago I had the occasion to see my 1947 movie *The Hucksters* with Clark Gable. I thought at the time that I looked mighty good. Of course, I was all of twenty-five ...

Robert: Huckster?

Ava: Ad people. Advertising. Guys paid to get you to buy something you don't need. It was a small part, but I loved it, being in a movie with Clark Gable, being his girlfriend. I have a copy of MGM's release of my statistics ...

Robert: Which were?

Ava: (*Smiling*) My, my. You are bad. Bust, thirty-five and three-quarters. Waist, as I recall, a bit more than twenty-three. Hips, thirty-four. You want to hear an inside Hollywood story?

Robert: Most assuredly.

Ava: The movie—*The Hucksters*—came from a best selling book. In the movie, my character, Jean Ogilvie, admits to paying more for her bras because of a mismatched pair—one breast slightly lower. When they put this in the movie, I raised hell. That would have stuck with me. Out it came.

Robert: Thank you ... that's enough about your movies. So, you are presently a Madrid neighbor of Ricardo and Betty Sicre. How well have you gotten to know them?

Ava: I met Ricardo first, at a party. Betty was in Morocco at the time. When Betty returned, we became great friends. Are you aware, we bought houses not far apart?

Robert: Yes, Ricardo mentioned this. We are in regular contact as he attempts to keep my business affairs in order.

Ava: (*Smiling*) Ricardo is also assisting me. He's attempting to get me to spend less then I earn ...

Robert: Betty said you will probably make Madrid your permanent home.

Ava: Yes, if—I should say, when—I divorce Frank. Madrid is far enough away from Hollywood to find peace.

Robert: Spain, of course, is quite different from America. Would it trouble you to live under a dictator?

Ava: I never gave it any thought. That is, until I couldn't get the damn bureaucrats to hook up my telephone. I cursed the guy and told him Franco could stick the phone you-know-where. Ricardo heard what I was saying and—honest-to-God— turned pale.

Robert: (*Frowning*) Well, he should. Ricardo is a Calonist, backed the Republic against Franco.

Ava: But didn't he become a US citizen during the war?

Robert: He did, but the Sicres, like the Graveses, and Ava Gardner, if she takes up residence, reside in Spain at the pleasure of Generalissimo Franco. He is a very sensitive leader, as are all dictators who see enemies on all sides ...

Ava: Ricardo feels that in time Spain will become a constitutional democracy under a monarch.

Robert: Yes, I agree with Ricardo. But only after Franco. Following World War II, our governments—the British and the Americans—were very unhappy with Franco. Our ambassadors were even withdrawn for a time.

Ava: Why?

Robert: When Franco rebelled against the leftist Spanish government, support came from Hitler and Mussolini. And while he kept Spain out of the war, he gave material support to Nazi Germany, even sending a division of so-called volunteers to fight the Soviets. At war's end, Franco aided Nazis seeking to escape retribution. Many found a home in Spain, others in South America, reportedly taking much stolen property with them, especially art and gold.

Ava: But that changed—we even have American air bases here.

Robert: The Cold War has altered relationships. Two years ago, Spain signed a treaty with the United States, thus allowing your country to build air and naval bases here in exchange for financial and military help. This keeps Franco in power, but I believe, also sets a course toward a Spanish democracy ... after Franco.

Ava: Thank you, Robert. I came for an education in poetry, only to be lectured on politics. Perhaps I should return and run for a senate seat in my home state of North Carolina.

Robert: Better stay with poetry. You'll find more enjoyment.

Ava: Poetry, it is. Besides, actors don't belong in Washington, so best I stay with the movies and enjoy poetry between takes.

Robert: I might share your opinion about actors as politicians, except for television. I see this spreading medium eventually turning politics into entertainment at the expense of substance. But of course, there will always be exceptions. Our Winston Churchill would have been quite successful as a character actor ... or should I say, was ...

Ava: Now that I've considered and abandoned a political career, tell me more about Ricardo and Betty. I've discovered, when not helping me with my Spanish, Ricardo is very sociable ... loves to entertain famous people on his yacht, the Rampager. He even introduced me to Adlai Stevenson, our guy at the UN. Have you known them long?

Robert: We met briefly in England in 1939, shortly before the war. We were both exiles from the Spanish Civil War. (*Smiling*) Ricardo tells many interesting tales from the war.

Ava: Not bloody ones, I hope.

Robert: Those are left unsaid. His best ones come with becoming an American spy.

Ava: Ah ... sounds exciting.

Robert: When your country entered the war, Ricardo offered his services as an espionage agent. It was called the OSS.

Ava: OSS?

Robert: Office of Strategic Services. They worked closely with Britain's. A spy agency.

Ava: Dangerous?

Robert: Yes, the danger came when he was posted to France as a counterintelligence agent. But this is not the story he prefers to tell at parties.

Ava: Errol Flynn stuff?

Robert: (*Smiling*) Yes, a bit. Ricardo was sent to America for training ... Washington.

Ava: A handsome and sexy Spaniard loose in a city of young ladies ...

Robert: Most certainly, as he tells it. The OSS wanted information from foreign governments, so Ricardo led an effort breaking into foreign embassies.

Ava: The German and Japanese embassies?

Robert: No, Ricardo's main target was the Spanish embassy, not surprising, as Franco favored the Axis.

Ava: Was he successful?

Robert: (*Smiling*) Very successful ... and this makes the story worth telling. It seems, the OSS gave him much money, which he used to seduce the embassy secretaries.

Ava: Ah ha! This, I can understand.

Robert: From the ladies, he gained enough information to enable him to break in at night to photograph documents.

Ava: (*Laughing*) Ah! The Errol Flynn connection. Tough duty.

Robert: It was followed with duty in North Africa, where he trained agents to cross from Spain into Vichy France. Later he, himself, went into France as a counterintelligence agent.

Ava: I understand Ricardo met Betty during the war. Was it in France or Spain?

Robert: France. Betty also was an American agent ... teaming-up with Ricardo. She is as much a remarkable person as her husband.

Ava: Now, that has the making of a great movie.

Robert: True, but it is unlikely to happen. Ricardo is a very successful businessman. Even though he is now an American citizen, he is not beyond the reach of Franco. Now, tell me about your career, which I find far more interesting. (*Smiles*) And, perhaps, even poetic.

Ava: I doubt that. I've been in bad films ... lately, much better. *Pandora and the Flying Dutchman* was filmed here in Spain. I enjoyed that. *Mogambo* led some to believe I could really act, that I was more than just a body. The critics said very nice things about my acting in *The Snows of Kiliman-jaro* and Papa Hemingway was pleased with the result.

Robert: I have heard—or perhaps read—that you prefer to swim nude.

Ava: (*Smiling*) In movies, no. Otherwise, yes.

Robert: (*He returns the smile.*) And that after you dived into his pool, our Mr. Hemingway directed the caretaker never to drain the water.

Ava: (*Laughing*) I hadn't heard that, and I'll bet it came from Betty Sicre by way of Ricardo who got it during bar talk with Hemingway. If true, it was a damn foolish thing for Papa to do ... I probably peed in his pool.

Robert: (*Smiling*) When the children insist on a visit to the beach, will you alter your preference and don appropriate attire?

Ava: I'll give it serious consideration, just this once. By the way, getting back to my stats, I once went swimming—in a bathing suit!—with Betty's boys. They are real Spaniards—and damn if one of them didn't filch my bra.

Robert: (*Smiling*) I assure you, our children are well-behaved. But best you do appear modest ... at least as long as you are in Deya. The natives are wonderful but quite old-fashioned. Now, shall we move onto poetry before the wonderful lunch my wife Beryl has in mind.

Ava: Please do ... on to poetry. I must confess, Robert, I really don't understand poetry. Betty has lent me her copy of the *Oxford Book of English Verse*. Some I like, most I just don't understand.

Robert: My dear. You're not supposed to understand poetry, you're supposed to enjoy it. It is words, not meaning, that is important. Words are a poet's riches. And always keep this in mind: poetry means a tremendous concentration of ideas. Have you been introduced to *The White Goddess*?

Ava: Only in passing. It was mentioned by Papa Hemingway, but no details.

Robert: I expected you might be unprepared. (*He takes a book from the side table.*) Here is a copy for you to keep. It is, I'm often told, a very difficult book. The muse, you'll come to understand— with my help—is the goddess of poetry. Poets are born, not made. Thus a poet needs to be devoted to the influence of a muse—a channel through which her unmediated inspiration can flow. (*Smiling*) Have I lost you?

Ava: (*Smiling*) Yes, but I feel we will be exploring the meaning of love ...

Robert: Yes ... in love, I have had several muses ... and a muse can be alluring but also potentially deadly. The muse can be a lovely women, but she can also revert to a witch, a she-wolf, a bitch, a sow, or other detested creature. And with this, your first lesson about true poetry must end. If we delay lunch, Beryl—though a most tolerant and gentle person, my favorite muse of the moment—might be unhappy.

Ava: (*Smiling*) I have heard that you favor young muses, and they can be quite expensive.

Robert: In pursuit of poetry, there can be no limit ...

Ava: ... and it will keep you young ...

Robert: (*Smiling*) Perhaps.

Ava: What I'm hearing is that a young muse—let me put it this way—it takes a young muse to stir your juices, to create poetry, of course.

Robert: (*Smiling*) And often it requires poetry to attract young muses!

Ava: What a wonderful circle, a wonderful way of staying alive.

Robert: It seems to be working.

Ava: (*In a light-hearted tone*) So a muse can be—how might I put it—whatever, even a poorly educated and lusty actress.

Robert: (*Equally light-hearted*) Quite possible, quite possible. And as I've gotten to know you, I realize we have met before.

Ava: (*Frowning*) We have?

Robert: Most assuredly. A muse can be mystically if not physically present.

Ava: You're moving beyond me. That word never surfaced in my school in North Carolina.

Robert: It means I once produced a poem inspired by a muse I couldn't identify. It was someone, I am now convinced, that had invaded my subconscious.

Ava: (*Smiling*) If you're pinning this on me, I insist you produce the poem.

Robert: (*Pointing*) Over there, in the bookcase. Second shelf, third from the left. Please bring me the book.

(*Ava produces the book as directed, handing it to Robert. He turns to a certain page.*)

Robert: Ah! Listen carefully, my metaphysical muse ... (*Begins reading.*)

THE PORTRAIT
She speaks always in her own voice
Even to strangers; but those other women
Exercise their borrowed, or take, voices
Even on sons and daughters.
She can walk invisibly at noon
Along the high road; but those other women
Gleam phosphorescent—broad hips and gross
    fingers—
Down every lampless alley.
She is wild and innocent, pledged to love
Through all disaster; but those other women
Decry her for a witch or a common drab
And glare back when she greets them.
Here is her portrait, gazing sidelong at me,
The hair is disarray, the young eyes pleading:
'And you, love? As unlike those other men
As I those other women?'

Ava: (*Quiet for a brief moment.*) Would you mind repeating that line that begins "She is wild and innocent"?

Robert: Yes, of course:
  She is wild and innocent, pledged to love
  Through all disaster, but those other women
  Decry her as a witch or a common drab ...

Ava: (*Interrupting*) That's enough. I believe I understand relating this to me. Please, may I have a copy? Perhaps, in time, I will understand the entire poem.

Robert: I'll have one before you depart.

(*Beryl enters the room.*)

Beryl: Lunch is ready if you two can spare the time.

Robert: Thank you, my dear.

(*They rise and Robert takes Ava's arm as they move toward the door.*)

Robert: Let me remind you, my long-missing muse, if young Lucia and Juan press you into service as an escort to the beach, you must be properly attired.

Ava: (*Laughing*) But of course, Robert. But you must find me a couple of your hankies to be—as you put it—properly attired!

Beryl: I'll not inquire into this ... (*They exit the stage laughing.*)

(*The characters leave the stage. The playwright enters the stage and addresses the audience.*)

Playwright: Let me add a postscript to the play. Robert Graves died in 1985 at the age of ninety. His voluminous papers are in the Robert Graves Trust Archives at St. John's College, Oxford. Summaries note the extensive correspondence between both Robert and his wife with Ricardo and Betty Sicre, the couple that introduced Robert and Ava. The archive also contains considerable correspondence between Robert and Ava. Ava died in London in 1990 at the age of sixty-nine. Graves's affection for Ava is revealed in his story "A Toast to Ava Gardner" published in *The New Yorker*, April 26, 1958. Other sources in developing the play included *Ernest Hemingway: A Life Story* by Carlos Baker, 1969; *Ava: My Story* by Ava Gardner, 1990; *Robert Graves: Life on the Edge* by Miranda Seymour, 1995; *Ava Gardner* by Lee Server, 2006; and *Ava Gardner: The Secret Conversations* by Peter Evans and Ava Gardner, 2013. I hope you enjoyed the conversation between Robert and Ava.

Ava, Robert, & Friends
essay

In 1955, the motion-picture star Ava Gardner departed her native country and took up residence in Madrid, Spain. This self-imposed exile was to distance herself from her estranged husband, Frank Sinatra, whom she had decided to divorce. She also had decided to settle in a place and a culture that she had come to admire, especially the music (flamenco) and the men (bullfighters).

Once settled in Madrid, Ava developed a close relationship with her neighbors, Ricardo and Betty Sicre. Both were US citizens, though born abroad. Ricardo was a native Spaniard, a Catalan from a province in northern Spain that includes Barcelona.

Betty was born in Canada but raised in Maryland. She achieved US citizenship through her parents. The Sicres provided the link connecting Robert Graves—the esteemed English poet and novelist, a permanent resident on the Spanish island of Mallorca (Majorca)—and the beautiful actress Ava Gardner, then in her early thirties.

Ricardo Sicre had fought on the side of the Loyalists in Spain's Civil War, a fact that led to his self-exile to England in 1939, following the defeat of the Soviet-supported republic by Generalissimo Francisco Franco. A chance encounter with Robert Graves—also self-exiled from his home in the village of Deya, Mallorca—led not only to an enduring friendship but also to Sicre becoming Graves's financial advisor. When America entered the war, Ricardo volunteered to serve with the US Office of Strategic Services (OSS), precursor to today's Central Intelligence Agency, as an espionage agent in occupied France, service that led to achieving American citizenship at the end of the Second World War.

Betty Sicre (nee, Lassier) earned her pilot's license at an early age, a skill offered to the British Royal Air Transport Service early in the war. Becoming bored, she sought a new role in the war. Her father had served in the Canadian Air Force in the First World War along with a flyer named William Stephenson. Stephenson came to head the British

Secret Intelligence Service. That connection gained Betty enlistment in the OSS and, in due course, a posting in German-occupied France, where she met, fell in love, and at war's end married fellow spy Ricardo Sicre.

With Ricardo having achieved US citizenship, the Sicres had no concern about dictator Franco seeking retribution against a Republic army officer that had fought against him. In the postwar decade, Ricardo's entrepreneurial talents would make the Sicres very wealthy and popular among Madrid's social set. Their yacht, the *Rampager*, would host many international celebrities, including Ernest and Mary Hemingway, the Prince and Princess of Monaco, Adlai Stevenson (then the US Ambassador to the United Nations), and, of course, Ava Gardner.

Robert and Ava first met in Madrid at a small party hosted by the Sicres. Graves was entranced by the beautiful actress, eager to engage her in conversation. He found, however, that she made it a point to avoid him, later learning that someone had wrongly identified him as a famous British scientist. (She was, I suspect, woefully untutored in all things scientific!) The Sicres set the matter straight and were instrumental in Ava visiting Robert and Beryl Graves at their home in Mallorca "for a badly needed rest from the whirl of social activities in Madrid."

Ava was warmly received upon arriving in Mallorca, not only by Robert but by his wife Beryl and their three small children. As for a "rest," Ava arrived, according to her biographer, "with a list drawn up of resolutions for Robert and his family to help implement: She must rest, swim in the sea, study Spanish grammar, and learn about poetry." (*Ava Gardner* by Lee Server, 2006.) In a *New Yorker* article, "A Toast to Ava Gardner," Robert confirmed this: "We had an unexpected [sic] visit from Ava Gardner, a close friend of our friend Betty Sicre. Betty suggested that Ava take a short holiday from the exhausting life of Madrid to visit soporific and truly rural Mallorca. There she could catch up on sleep, study Spanish grammar, swim daily, and consult me about how to finish her random education by a crash-course in English poetry." Most accounts of the visit indicate that some but not all of the "resolutions" were accomplished. Ava stirred up as much attention in the villages as in Madrid, being constantly followed by adoring Spaniards, especially young men.

How might one tell the story of the visit between Robert and Ava? Some details are available, though much would have to be created, suggesting a fictionalized short story. Another approach would be to present the visit in a one-act play, the approach finally chosen.

Crucial to creating a play is to develop the action and dialog to fit the characters being represented: Robert Graves, the intellectual and master of the English language; Ava Gardner as an intelligent but undereducated American primitive not at all bashful about seeding her language with bits of profanity, be it in public or private conversations.

Before embarking on developing the play, it was essential to research the lives of the two characters. Fortunately, both are the subject of excellent biographies: *Robert Graves: Life on the Edge* by Miranda Seymour (1995) and *Ava Gardner: Love Is Nothing* by Lee Server (2006). Both Robert and Ava had published autobiographies, but not unlike most, they are self-serving and contain serious omissions and errors of fact. One source leaned upon heavily was *Conversations with Robert Graves*, edited by Frank L. Kersnowski (1989).

As noted earlier, the conversation between Robert and Ava took place in Graves's home when Ava came for her first visit with Robert and his wife Beryl and their children, a visit arranged by Ricardo and Betty Sicre.

Introducing the Sicres as the link between Robert and Ava required that they be described early in the play. It was also decided to introduce Ernest Hemingway into the conversation, but not in person. Hemingway was known to both Robert and Ava and had met the Sicres. Both as a novelist and short-story writer, Hemingway contributed to screen plays featuring Ava, the most popular being the *The Sun Also Rises*.

Robert and Ava: An Intimate Conversation Between the Poet Robert Graves and The Actress Ava Gardner was read by PlayReaders audience on March 17, 2011, and was well received. The continuing interest in Ava Gardner continued with details of her final days in London, included in *Ava Gardner: The Secret Conversations* by Peter Evans and Ava Gardner (2013).

Robert and Ava may never make it to Broadway, but the research and writing was and is quite stimulating and has left the playwright with great respect for two very flawed but very captivating characters.

Exploitation

Dawn of the Cold War

A History Play

Exploitation reveals a little-known aspect of the post-World War Two exploitation of German military technology and employment of German technologists. It is intended to be performed but is equally effective with a staged reading and discussion.

Introduction

The Allied invasion of Nazi Germany was closely followed by teams dedicated to exploiting advanced technology—mostly, but not limited to, military-related equipment. The American military led the effort with highly organized teams: The Navy (Naval

Technical Mission-Europe), Army Air Forces (Project Lusty), and Army Ordnance (Special Mission V2).

The V2 (originally designated the A4 but later changed to V2 with the "V" for *vergeltungswaffe*, translated as "reprisal weapon") was a supersonic rocket, forty-six feet long, weighing more than thirteen tons, had a range of 225 miles, and carried a one-ton warhead.

As American forces advanced into Germany, small, highly mobilized intelligence units called "T Forces" were close behind, ready to identify and guard coveted equipment and related documents. One such unit followed the capture of Nordhausen in Central Germany and the underground facility producing the V2. They also liberated Camp Dora, a concentration camp housing slave laborers provided by the SS from the nearby Buchenwald concentration camp.

Act One is set in May 1945 when the T-Force officer left to guard the Mittelwerk rocket factory and the Dora-Mittelbau concentration camp is visited by the two officers of Special Mission V2 who have been ordered to locate and ship to the United States one hundred rockets for evaluation and testing and possibly for actual use in the expected invasion of Japan. Act One opens as the officers arrive. Act Two covers the arrival of two members of the Naval

Technical Mission, one being Charles A. Lindbergh, Jr., a civilian attached to the mission. Act Three focuses on the conflict between exploiting German technology and prosecuting war criminals.

The play follows actual events. When American combat units overran the German rocket facility, they discovered thousands of dead and dying slave laborers, eventually estimating that upwards of twenty thousand had actually died of starvation, disease, beatings, and executions. A war crimes investigation parallels the exploitation effort but fails to directly implicate the leaders of the rocket program.

As a military weapon, the Nazi ballistic rocket was an expensive failure in lives and treasure. But, as historian Michael Neufeld noted in his outstanding study *The Rocket and the Reich* (1995), "It was the grandfather of all guided missiles and space boosters."

The Cast
(in order of appearance)

Donald O'Neil: Young. Wears Army OD uniform with the rank of sergeant. Walks with a pronounced limp.

Harry Fuller: About forty. Army uniform with the rank of lieutenant colonel. Medium-sized, but slightly overweight. A former judge that has the manner of a "good old boy" with a sharp intellect.

James "Jim" Harper: Twenty-six, regular army major in charge of Special Mission V2. A graduate of Fordham University with a degree in physics. Armed with a .45 Colt.

William "Bill" Bronson: Major in the army ordnance corps. About the same age as Harper. Engineering graduate. Also armed.

Ben Wilder: Major army intelligence on assignment to the war crimes unit. An attorney in civilian life. Late twenties.

Charles A. Lindbergh, Jr.: A noted aviator; a civilian assigned to the Naval Technical Mission Europe.

Ernst Kroeler: A naval lieutenant detailed to accompany Lindbergh.

Philip Michaud: A French civilian brought to Camp Dora as forced labor. Late thirties, but appears older.

Boll: A German in his late forties.

Act One

The stage is set as a small office. It is equipped with two small desks and tables and several chairs. On one desk is the name plate Lt. Col. Fuller, the second the name Sgt. O'Neil. Behind O'Neil is a table with a radio and a stack of file folders. On the wall is a map and a chart. As the scene opens O'Neil is reading a copy of the Army's *Stars and Stripes* newspaper and listening to music. (For a staged performance, a copy of *Stars and Stripes* with the headline "HITLER DEAD" is at the end of this play to be reproduced in appropriate size). When Fuller enters, O'Neil stands.

O'Neil: Sir!

Fuller: Relax, sergeant. And leave the radio. We're due a proclamation from General Eisenhower, one I expect you will enjoy hearing.

O'Neil: (*Smiling*) I've already got two bets laid ...

Fuller: If I didn't keep you occupied, you'd probably find your way to HQ to write the proclamation.

O'Neil: Only if so ordered, sir!

(*The music stops, and a voice is heard.*)

Radio Announcer: We are interrupting the regular scheduled program of the Armed Forces Network to bring you a special announcement from Supreme Allied Headquarters. General Eisenhower, today, May 8, 1945, issued the following proclamation: In 1943 the late President Roosevelt and Prime Minister Churchill met in

Casablanca. There they pronounced the formula
of unconditional surrender of the Axis Powers.
In Europe that formula has now been fulfilled.
The Allied force, which invaded Europe on June
6, 1944, has, with its great Russian ally and the
forces advancing from the south, utterly defeat-
ed the Germans on land, sea, and air. To every
subordinate that has been in this command of
almost 5,000,000 Allies, I owe a debt of gratitude
that can never be repaid. The only repayment
that can be made to them is deep appreciation
and lasting gratitude of all the free citizens of all
the United Nations. We will now return to our
regular program.

*(O'Neil turns off the radio. For a staged performance, a
tape recording of General Eisenhower's speech can be ob-
tained from the Eisenhower Library, Abilene, Kansas.)*

O'Neil: Well, Colonel. If you will excuse me, I'll be
off to start packing. The chicks in Prairie Junc-
tion need me now that General Ike doesn't.

Fuller: No doubt, Sergeant, your service to those
lovely ladies will be more enjoyable than that
you provided General Eisenhower. However,
I'm certain the general would appreciate your
services a mite longer. We've but three weeks
before Ivan moves in and much remains to be
done; hopefully by the ordnance team due any
minute.

O'Neil: (*Smiling*) Well, sir, I guess the ladies can suffer a bit longer ... and I hear a jeep, which spells ordnance. If you'll permit me, I'll check ...

Fuller: Welcome the gentlemen with open arms, Sergeant.

(*As Fuller awaits the ordnance officers, he focuses on the wall charts. As O'Neil enters with two officers, Fuller offers his hand.*)

Fuller: Gentlemen. Harry Fuller. Welcome.

Harper: Colonel. Jim Harper.

Fuller: Jim ... let's keep it informal. We'll be doing a lot of work together. (*Turns to the second officer and offers his hand.*) Major ...

Bronson: Colonel ... Bill Bronson.

Fuller: Bill. Gentlemen, let's sit and review what we have ahead of us. (*Turning to O'Neil.*) Meanwhile, perhaps the sergeant can scrounge some coffee. And Sergeant, not that kind served in the officer's mess. Can you manage a decent brew I know you're getting in the enlisted mess?

O'Neil: (*Smiling*) Yessir! The mess sergeant knows I appreciate good coffee. I'll be toot sweet! (*Departs*)

Fuller: Were you able to hear Eisenhower's proclamation?

Harper: No, but we heard about the signing of the German surrender, and it was expected after Hitler's death but nice to get the official word.

Fuller: Right. But here is a directive from the US Joint Chiefs of Staff just relayed from General Eisenhower that you might have missed. Dated 24 April 1945, it reads: Preserve from destruction and take under control records, plans, books, documents, paper, files, and scientific, industrial, and other information and data belonging to German organizations engaged in military research.

Bronson: We were alerted that something like this was on the way. That's as all-inclusive as it can get. Anything that aided the German war effort is to be exploited. This is our understanding.

Fuller: Right. And my alert to your visit read "Top Priority." I've placed a twenty-four-hour guard on all rockets, including those out of the tunnels. If three or four will fill your order, loading those outside will prove the easiest.

Bronson: (*Smiling, as was Harper*) Were it so easy. Our orders, from a boss that never takes "no" for an answer, are to ship one hundred, in whole or in part.

Fuller: Holy cow! I had you figured for a few .. then the rest destroyed. But you ask, you get. I hope they aren't due to go far.

Bronson: Well, a bit of a ways. By rail to Antwerp, ship to New Orleans, rail to El Paso, then north to an army base in New Mexico. It's my duty all the way.

Fuller: Well, my count is that you have the one hundred ... in whole or mostly in parts. And Nordhausen has the rail stock. Sea travel ... you're on your own. About the rail. This I anticipated, though not the number. The army transportation people riding herd on all rail stock in Nordhausen have orders to begin moving the lot north to Leipzig.

Bronson: Guess we'll have to pull rank.

Fuller: Reading "Top Priority" for your project, I contacted the officer in charge and found him unpersuaded to give you first call on what you might require. It seems someone, probably the air force, has some hot items scrounged from the Göring Aeronautical Institute. However, it happens that the only line north crosses a bridge that has collapsed—no doubt damaged by Allied bombs. We'll load what you require and, as you know, the Soviets are due to take over this area as part of the occupation zone. And, I might add, a couple of Russian officers have been snooping...

Harper: To be expected. The deal cut for the occupation zones stipulates that all German hardware stay in place. Signed with fingers crossed, no doubt. We passed through Stuttgart—it will be in the US zone—and the French were moving out entire factories. The Russians get what we leave.

Fuller: (*Laughing*) The Russians aren't the only ones who covet what we have. A British colonel here a couple of days ago wanted a count on the rockets. I said I'd get around to it.

Bronson: Figures. The four-zone arrangement also included a separate deal with the Brits to div-vy-up—we get half, they get half. Well, their half will be in New Mexico. Which is why we want to load and get on our way. As soon as they know we're on the move, no doubt they will take it to the highest level to get their cut.

(*O'Neil enters with coffee.*)

O'Neil: Sorry, gentlemen ... Colonel Fuller, Major Wilder just arrived.

Fuller: Good. Invite him to join us.

O'Neil: Yessir.

(*O'Neil departs.*)

Fuller: Major Wilder was the intelligence officer with the regiment that liberated this place. He is now detailed to a war crimes unit. He's gung-ho about bringing to justice the Germans involved here ... and since we're nearing lunch time, you might appreciate a little background on the

tunnel complex and Dora. Meanwhile, I'll start
the ball rolling on what you'll need.

(*O'Neil enters with Major Wilder.*)

Fuller: Nice to see you, Ben. Ben, Jim Harper
and Bill Bronson. (*They shake hands.*) Sergeant
O'Neil, will you set the four of us for lunch?
And while you are here … what do you know
about the collapse of the rail bridge twenty miles
north?

O'Neil: (*Smiling*) Well, sir, talk was it was in pretty
bad shape. Didn't believe that so I bet Sergeant
Holly—he's the ordnance guy blowing up German stuff—that the bridge was solid as a rock.

Fuller: And the bet … ?

O'Neil: Well, sir, as it happens, I had run across a
supply of wine the Nazis had stashed down the
road … and Major Wilder's guys overlooked.
(*Smiles*) I bet the sergeant a case of really fine
stuff, and darn if he didn't win. Can't figure out
why that darn bridge decided to collapse.

Fuller: Well, Sergeant O'Neil, to be certain that
you didn't take advantage of the sergeant, why
don't you add a bottle to our lunch?

O'Neil: Yes sir! I know you'll appreciate the quality.
I'll see that lunch is ready within a half hour.
Gentlemen. (*Departs*)

(*The men are smiling.*)

Fuller: When I write my memoir telling how the war was won, I'll give deserved credit to young soldiers like the sergeant. That limp he carries bought not only a Purple Heart but also the Silver Star at Bastogne. He could have been invalided home, but he said he told his daddy he wouldn't come home 'til the Nazis cried uncle.

Harper: That's been my experience. GI's gripe about the army, but when the chips are down, they produce.

Fuller: He probably heard me talking about how important it was to have that rail stock ready to move west, not north. The result figures. One more point about our project ... (*Goes to the wall and points to a drawing of the tunnels.*) After lunch I'll take you on a tour to see what you have. (*Points*) Each of these side tunnels had a rocket in various stages of completion. With overhead hoists in place, it will be easy to load when the train is backed into the tunnel. And no problem with labor. I've a camp full of German POWs. All I have to do is to suggest they will be relocated west before the Russians take over. They'll work like hell.

Harper: (*Smiling*) You do offer a nice incentive. Sounds like a much easier chore than we expected.

Bronson: (*Addressing Wilder*) Major, I expect you're as busy as the two of us. What's the story here? Got the bad guys rounded up?

Wilder: (*Smiling*) One positive note is that the Krauts did keep excellent records, which they conveniently left behind. What wasn't left behind were the bad guys. Besides this camp, Camp Dora, there are thirty-one sub-camps. And in Nordhausen, there is a large former military camp that received those workers no longer able to work.

This is what the Third Armored Division first encountered. We've estimated it took about a thousand SS to control the prisoners. We have fourteen in custody, of which but nine are SS, the others are German Kapos, common criminals who aided the SS.

Harper: How in hell did so many manage to get away?

Wilder: First you have to accept that the SS was determined that none of the forced workers would survive. We've confirmed this from junior SS officers in custody. About a thousand workers were still quite healthy, and these were sent north to Bergen-Belsen, a camp still in German hands. They had to be guarded by a couple hundred SS guards. Others, when they heard our troops coming, faded into the civilian population—along with German civilian workers—or changed their SS uniforms for regular army.

Bronson: If they left good records, couldn't you track some down?

Wilder: We hope so, but I believe this was carefully planned, and they have bona fide Wehrmacht identification.

Bronson: How about the thousand prisoners moved north? Were they liberated?

Wilder: Second only to the treatment of Jews, this has to stand as one of the worst Nazi atrocities. They were locked in a barn that was set on fire ...

Bronson: Good God! All thousand?

Wilder: Our troops were nearby, and several did manage to escape and confirm what happened. The SS guards did get away, but we have the name of the SS officer in charge and hope to eventually have him in custody.

Harper: Major Wilder, have you been able to ascertain who was in charge? Who at the very top ought to be held accountable?

Wilder: Yes. We have three SS lieutenants in custody, plus one captain. By the way, the Nazis have done us one favor: SS have their blood type tattooed under their left arm. POWs in camps in the area are being checked, and I hope we'll uncover a few missing guards. Anyway, the SS officers have been a wealth of information, especially in identifying the ranking SS general, a person so bad even his subordinates hated his guts.

Fuller: (*Smiling*) The infamous SS Brigadeführer Dr. Hans Kammler ...

Wilder: Exactly. Himmler's man to execute the SS role in the rocket program. The SS provided the slave labor ...

Fuller: Good choice of word—"execute."

Wilder: Harry captured the essence of Kammler. In a nation without a conscience, Kammler ranks with Himmler and Hitler. One of the prisoners, Philip Michaud, a French professor, has been assisting me with details of Dora and translations. A group of French prisoners who still believed some Germans retained a touch of humanity decided to appeal to Kammler. He agreed to hear them out. Their spokesman explained they understood they must work but pleaded for better food and a curb on the constant beatings. Kammler heard them out, nodded, wherein his two SS guards opened fired with machine pistols. Eighty of the prisoners died.

Bronson: Good Lord! Most of us accept that every Dr. Jekyll has a bit of Mr. Hyde inside that must be controlled. But this guy appears to be 100 percent Hyde and relishes the character. Has he ... or can he be caught?

Wilder: All we know is that Himmler promoted him and gave him command of an SS division at Prague. G2 reports that captured SS officers say his aide was to shoot him to prevent capture by the Soviets. Did it happen? We don't know. Another report has him fleeing Prague with a group of SS officers, only to be strafed by a Thunderbolt fighter with all killed. No confirmation. Incidentally, he has been described as the one who directed the construction of Auschwitz—a very resourceful person.

Harper: Learning what you're up against, I'm glad I decided not to take up the law. Looking for rockets is much easier than rounding up the Kammlers. As for rocket experts, I interviewed several, and they assured me that working conditions weren't all that bad—harsh but, considering wartime conditions, pretty good...

Wilder: And you believed the Krauts?

Harper: It is not my responsibility to believe or not believe. My job was to assess the technical expertise of those in custody. As for what they said about the workers in the factory, I passed up the line what I had been told.

Wilder: Well, I hope those "up the line" are interested in justice being done. We've not done too well in identifying the civilians that ran this version of hell. One in charge, a guy named Sawatzke, was killed by prisoners before the army got control. Another, an engineer named Georg Rickhey, was the last person in charge, and we believe we have a lead on him. My main task is to interview the same guys who gave you a cock-and-bull story. Any help you can give will be most appreciated—not just by me, but by the poor souls who suffered.

Harper: (*As O'Neil enters*) I'll see that this is passed on to Colonel Toftoy, who runs Special Mission V2 out of Paris. I'm certain he'll cooperate.

Wilder: One more thing … Sergeant O'Neil, can you pull the draft of the *Third Armored Division History*?

O'Neil: Yessir, no problem. (*Goes to the cabinet, pulls a file, and hands it to Wilder.*)

Wilder: I helped draft the *Third Armored Division History*. Let me read a brief section that describes what we encountered when we captured this place on April 11. "Hundreds of corpses lay sprawled over the acres of the big compound. More hundreds filled the great barracks. They lay in contorted heaps, half stripped, mouths gaping in the dirt and straw, or they were piled naked, like cordwood in the corners and under the stairwell…" We have photographs to confirm.

Harper: Yes, Major. I accept the Germans I Interviewed preferred to remember things quite differently.

Wilder: The *Stars and Stripes* carried a story a couple of weeks ago claiming some 22,000 slaves worked here until we got close and they shut down. In fact, we have estimated the total since the factory became operational in the fall of 1943 was nearly 60,000, of which an estimated 20,000 died from mistreatment, disease, and executions. We also had a congressional delegation visit on April 23, and I'm looking forward to their report.

Fuller: Gentlemen, I hope this hasn't ruined your lunch, but it is what must be faced. You'll come to grips with it again when you get into the factory ...

O'Neil: Colonel Fuller, gentlemen ... lunch is served if you follow me.

Act Two

Act Two is set in a separate and more sparse office at Camp Dora. Furnishings include a desk, table, several chairs, and several filing cabinets. There are a stack of cards on the table and two lengths of cable. Lindbergh, Kroeler, and O'Neil enter. It is two weeks following the visit of the ordnance officers from Special Mission V2.

O'Neil: This was the SS sergeant's office. He kept the records. A JAG officer has been using it ... You know, war crimes stuff.

Lindbergh: (*Sniffing the air*) Mousey! That's it, mousey! I've smelled it in every building and in the tunnels. I remember it from the farm. Mice! They nest and the smell lingers. Mousey!

O'Neil: The stink? That's death, Colonel. The stink of death. You can remove the bodies, but the stink stays. (*Smiles*) I guess we've gotten sorta used to it.

Kroeler: Well, I hope we're not around long enough. This place gives me the creeps.

Lindbergh: (*Selecting several cards from the table*) What are these?

O'Neil: Prisoner ID cards. The SS sarge had a card for every prisoner, dead or alive ... even if they had died at the first roll call. Name was Otto Brinkman. We have his daily reports. The Krauts are champion record keepers, and Otto was one of the best ... and the nastiest. Prisoners say roll call could last four or five hours. Otto had to balance his books. That's how investigators know how many came and how many died.

Kroeler: And how many was that, Sergeant?

O'Neil: Well ... sir. Maybe 60,000 worked here. Digging tunnels, making rockets, and flying bombs ... They say a third died.

Lindbergh: (*Incredulous*) Twenty thousand died!

O'Neil: Yeah, not many of the diggers made it. That musta been real bad. That's from one of the engineers who helped the ordnance guys clean out the rockets a couple of weeks ago. (*Pauses*) I guess Colonel Fuller will fill you in ...

Lindbergh: (*Smiling*) That's OK, sergeant. We know the army was here leaving nothing for the navy ... or the Russians. No worry. We all work for the same government. About the workers ...

O'Neil: You mean the prisoners?

Lindbergh: How about the Germans that ran the place? The engineers and technicians—any still around?

O'Neil: No, sir. According to Major Wilder ... He's the war crime's investigator ... He was with Third Armored that liberated Dora and the underground plant. The Krauts skedaddled as the SS moved out. Guess they were scared shit ... 'scuse me, Colonel! Guess they were worried about what the prisoners might do. Or maybe that they'd be arrested. Major Wilder ... he's a lawyer ... says the lot of 'em will be brought up on war crimes charges. Me ... I hope the lot of 'em get hung!

Lindbergh: He's Jewish?

O'Neil: Major Wilder? Gosh, Colonel. I don't rightly know. Never gave it a thought. But he sure is a nice guy ... sorry ... "officer."

Lindbergh: (*Shuffling through the cards.*) French, Polish, Russians, Hungarians ... Here's an Italian. Appears the Germans recruited workers from wherever they could.

O'Neil: "Shanghai" is a better word. Just like in *Mutiny on the Bounty* and Captain Bligh. One of the French prisoners told Major Wilder that the SS employed a whole lot of French gals who got paid to get guys liquored so they could be arrested and shipped to a kommando ...

Kroeler: Commando?

O'Neil: That's "Kommando" with a "K." German word for a labor camp like Dora. The major said prisoners claim two Americans flyers worked and died here, but so far no records to confirm. The major also found records on prisoners as young as twelve ... thirteen ...

Kroeler: (*Taking an object from the table.*) Look at this ... a length of heavy-duty electrical cable ... (*Slams it on the table.*)

O'Neil: (*Picks up a length of cable.*) That's for a routine blow. This—four feet of bare wire fitted with a handle—we're told by a prisoner that the SS used it to punish ... like being late for muster ... or dropping a rocket part ... even for stealing or receiving a piece of bread from a German worker. Says the SS used a stool. (*Gets a small stool from the corner.*) Here's one Major Wilder is saving for evidence. At muster, the prisoner would have to drop his pants and kneel down. Here, like this. (*Kneels with his stomach on the stool.*) The SS guard would whack the guy's butt while the poor guy kept count. Twenty-five whacks was the standard, but we're told most passed out after ten or twelve.

Lindbergh: (*Addressing Kroeler*) Lieutenant, to speed things up so we can move on, why don't you drive over to where a jet bomber was reported. Meanwhile, I'll stay here and make a few notes for our report.

Kroeler: Aye, aye, Colonel. (*Departs*)

Lindbergh: (*Smiling*) I keep reminding him that I am a civilian assigned to the naval technical mission. Guess I'm doomed to always be a colonel.

O'Neil: (*Has replaced the stool.*) Yessir ... My daddy always called you "Colonel."

Lindbergh: Sergeant, do you by chance have access to a barber? I am badly in need of a trim.

O'Neil: Yessir. We found one in the village, and he's pretty good. I can have him here pronto.

Lindbergh: Do that, Sergeant, and it will be most appreciated.

O'Neil: And Colonel, the going rate is three cigarettes. Best you don't overpay and jump up the price.

Lindbergh: I'll keep that in mind. (*O'Neil departs and Lindbergh takes out a notebook and proceeds to write. Suddenly he hears a noise, jumps up, reaches for his sidearm, and shouts.*) Who's there?

Michaud: (*Voice from off stage.*) My apologies!

(*Michaud, a small, gaunt man, emerges from off stage. He is dressed in army fatigues.*)

Michaud: I am Professor Phillip Michaud, a French citizen. I am returning SS documents that Major Wilder requested me to translate.

Lindbergh: (*Offering his hand.*) Charles Lindbergh, professor.

Michaud: Lindbergh! I am honored, Colonel.

Lindbergh: Please, professor, let's be comfortable (*They sit and Lindbergh continues.*) Actually, it's not "colonel." I'm a civilian advisor attached to the US Naval Technical Mission headquartered in Paris. You were, I gather, one of the Mittelwerk workers?

Michaud: Yes, an involuntary worker for the Third Reich.

Lindbergh: Yes, I understand conditions were terribly grim. You've delayed returning home ... back to France?

Michaud: Yes, I remained to care for a friend. He died last night. He was one of my students, a young man of nineteen with great promise ...

Lindbergh: I'm sorry.

Michaud: I will return his ashes to his family as soon as possible, hopefully within days. That is, if your Major Wilder is no longer in need of my services.

Lindbergh: You're assisting in the war crimes investigation?

Michaud: Yes, as much as possible. I speak German, some Polish. I've assisted with depositions, translations ... and, of course, what I know of Dora ... of Mittelwerk.

Lindbergh: How is it you came here? Were you a prisoner of war, as I understand were many of the laborers here?

Michaud: I was a prisoner of war but only briefly, in 1940. In April of last year, at my college in Lyon, I was arrested by the Germans and sent to Buchenwald.

Lindbergh: Are you Jewish?

Michaud: No!

Lindbergh: A communist?

Michaud: (*Smiling*) Briefly ... as a young student. I am a socialist.

Lindbergh: Resistance?

Michaud: Sympathetic, but not active. I was released by the Germans in early 1941, mustered out, and returned to my profession of teaching mathematics. Yes, Colonel, any one of those could get a Frenchman arrested and deported to Germany. But the Nazi reach was wide ...

Lindbergh: Do you know why you were arrested ... deported?

Michaud: Yes, I believe I know. During my initial interrogation, when I insisted I had said and done nothing against the Third Reich, the SS officer smiled and said, "Ah! But you are quite capable, are you not?" We—my group of deportees—were of the educated class—teachers, lawyers, engineers ... (*Smiles*) Except for a few Jews, our badge at Buchenwald was a red triangle signifying "political enemy." We were a threat to the Third Reich, not for what we had done—at least, most of us—but for what we were.

Lindbergh: You said you were first sent to Buchenwald. How many comprised your group ... the number from France?

Michaud: The shipment numbered some fifteen hundred. All men, though some, like my former student, Paul, were still boys.

Lindbergh: And how many, if you know, survived?

Michaud: Perhaps fifty; maybe seventy-five. Certainly, less than one hundred.

Lindbergh: Less than ten percent!

Michaud: It was more than the Germans expected. One does not survive a combination of hard labor, starvation, and constant brutality. We quickly came to accept the reality of our greeting by a SS sergeant: "You will not leave here alive ... I will see to this." That first roll call. In cold—very cold—weather ... lasted nearly four hours. Many collapsed, and some died of pneumonia. Later we spoke of them as "fortunate." Their suffering was brief.

Lindbergh: This was here? At Dora?

Michaud: When we arrived, there was no Camp Dora. Prisoners went directly into the tunnels where the floor beside our work station was our bed. The dampness and foul air claimed many lives. It was in June ... June of last year ... 1944 ...

that the SS put prisoners to work building what was to be the final home for many: Dora.

Lindbergh: The work in the tunnel ... on the rockets ... what was it like? Did conditions improve as production began?

Michaud: Our liberators ... your soldiers ... know the answer by what they found. Hundreds of corpses and the living dead. Each day there were new dead, most from malnutrition, disease, lung failure. The tunnels were damp and dirty and a work day was twelve hours. We were provided little water and scant rest. Our food was two bowls of watery soup, occasionally with a piece of unidentified meat. Many died of untreated injuries. Beatings were frequent. Executions less so, but increased with pressure for greater production.

Lindbergh: Sabotage?

Michaud: Any mechanical problem often was attributed to sabotage.

Lindbergh: Some truth?

Michaud: Some ... yes. When it was rumored that rockets had landed in Paris, I myself saw one of my compatriots urinate on a control mechanism. But sabotage had a broad meaning to the SS. Two Polish workers were executed for fashioning crude spoons from scrap metal.

Lindbergh: Executed—for that?

Michaud: Yes. The German foreman who caught them called an SS guard. He hanged them over their machines.

Lindbergh: Hanged them! Just like that? On his own authority?

Michaud: Yes, Colonel. Just like that. You must understand—here, SS guards, even German technicians and managers, had absolute life or death power over all prisoners. We were in a very literal sense slaves, chattel. We were owned by the SS, rented out to Mittelwerk. Unlike your American slaves of the last century, however, we held little value. Many died, but replacements came in due course. Perhaps we were considered the least costly of the Nazi war machine. Besides, having been judged as enemies of the Third Reich, we were doomed to die.

Lindbergh: Did many ... did any, manage to escape?

Michaud: No, not really. Not from Dora. At least at the end ... from Nordhausen, like myself.

Lindbergh: You escaped ... from Nordhausen?

Michaud: Yes. Those no longer able to work were taken to a special camp to await death. I was sent along to unload the dead and helpless and feed the crematorium. But perhaps I should spare you the details.

Lindbergh: No ... unless you find it too painful, please continue.

Michaud: Yes, perhaps I should. My history professor once said that keeping memory alive is very important to a civilized society. You Americans, especially, must come to believe the unbelievable ... Do you not agree?

Lindbergh: Yes, And I most certainly agree with your professor.

Michaud: Good! The Boelcke-Kaserne—the name of an old military barracks in the center of Nordhausen, now surrounded by barb wire and guarded by the SS. All prisoners sick and dying. Roll call twice a day. The dead collected for the crematorium. Your bombers came; the SS ran for the shelters. I was unhurt but very weak, exhausted, barely able to move. A young prisoner ... I believe he was Polish ... helped me. Outside, we found a supply of food and hid in a bomb crater, pulling debris over us. We waited ... days ... our food ran out, and the young man went to seek more. I never saw him again. Then I heard voices in English. Delirium? It was April 11. I made as much noise as I could, and soon the debris was pulled away. Men climbed down and pulled me out. I had survived Dora! I was in the care of civilized men.

Lindbergh: Were you able to learn the names of the Americans?

Michaud: One. He was Major Wilder, and we were able to meet again.

Lindbergh: The JAG officer, the war crimes investigator. Sergeant O'Neil mentioned that he was using this office.

Michaud: Yes. Perhaps now you understand why I remain to assist.

Lindbergh: Yes, and I commend you.

Michaud: Thank you.

Lindbergh: Professor, you were first taken to Buchenwald, a camp receiving much recent publicity. Was it worse than Dora?

Michaud: Can you compare any two of Dante's infernos? Yes, I witnessed more suffering here ... more brutality ... more dying. Yet, it was Buchenwald that remains engraved in my memory. It was there, when I was still strong, in good health, even hopeful, that I came to realize that, to the Nazis ... to the SS ... we were enemy, that we were not meant to survive ...

Lindbergh: Please understand how difficult it is for me to accept, to understand. I have visited Germany. I admire many Germans ... their culture ... their technology.

Michaud: Yes, I too have admired the Germans. Before the war I was a student at Leipzig University, and I have had many Germans as students. This, I suppose, added to my bewilderment at our treatment.

Lindbergh: Yes, please continue with your experience at Buchenwald.

Michaud: When we arrived, in a large room, we were ordered to remove our clothes. With a few blows from guards, we were made to form lines, an inmate barber at each. Our heads were shorn. All hair—heads, backs, chests, legs, crotch, and butt. Fifteen hundred totally naked men! We joked ... some laughed ... and were beaten. Then the realization set in: They could do to us whatever they wanted. Our humanity was left at the door to Buchenwald. This is why we understood the words spoken at Dora: "You will not leave here alive."

Lindbergh: The SS—they were in charge here at Dora?

Michaud: Yes, the SS was in charge. They ran Dora supported by selected prisoners called "kapos"—most German, common criminals. They performed no hard labor and received extra food. A few were decent ... most very brutal ... usually showing off to the SS.

Lindbergh: And the factory. Who ran Mittelwerk?

Michaud: Rocket assembly was directed by German civilians. The SS served as guards, underground as well as at Dora and the many subcamps ...

Lindbergh: Am I to understand that the SS played no role in producing the rockets?

Michaud: How much, I do not know. I do know of involvement, however. One day—late last year—several German civilians came by with an SS major and paused near me, and I was able to hear much of their conversation. Yes, my German is quite adequate. I, as required, had removed my cap and stood with my head bowed. I, to them, was a nonperson ... not seen ...

Lindbergh: Before you lowered your head, were you able to identify any of the group?

Michaud: Two civilians I had seen often—one the civilian in charge, the other in charge of production and addressed as Herr Rudolf. He was often on the assembly line.

Lindbergh: And the SS officer?

Michaud: Unusual! He was not addressed as "Major." He addressed Rudolf as "Arthur," and Rudolf addressed him as "Wernher." The other civilian addressed him as "Professor."

Lindbergh: No last name?

Michaud: No.

Lindbergh: Very interesting. Do you recall anything of their conversation?

Michaud: The SS major was complaining about the slow production, said pressure for more rockets was coming from the Führer. He also said that too many rockets were malfunctioning—over half—and that he planned to go to Buchenwald personally to select better workers. At that, they moved on.

Lindbergh: Any results you know about from the visit of the SS major?

Michaud: (*Smiling*) More beatings to speed up the production line. Yes, within a week we had many new prisoners, mostly French, some Dutch. One was a compatriot, Henri Garon, a man I knew. He related to me he was interviewed at Buchenwald by a very formal but polite SS major. Yes, by the description, it was the same SS officer. He questioned Garon at length about his education and experience: engineering. And very unusual, he did not require the prisoner to lower his head with eyes averted.

Lindbergh: Then he managed a good look at him.

Michaud: Yes. He described him as tall, light hair, blue eyes. Had the bearing of the German aristocracy.

Lindbergh: And the present whereabouts of your compatriot Mr. Garon?

Michaud: We do not know. Major Wilder has undertaken an intense search ... to no avail. I am afraid he was one of those marched to the north shortly before your soldiers arrived. Major Wilder says they were headed to a kommando in the north still in German hands.

(*There is noise off-stage, and O'Neil enters with a man in civilian clothes.*)

O'Neil: Pardon, Colonel Lindbergh, Professor. This is Herr Boll, said to be the best barber—or, maybe the only barber left around these parts. (*Lowers his voice.*) Remember Colonel, three cigarettes is the going rate. Says he's no Nazi and never liked Der Führer, which fits 'em all (*Turns to Boll.*) Herr Boll! You give the colonel your best haircut, and when you're finished you wait just outside this building ... No wandering about. Verstanzig?

Boll: Ya! Ya! I wait.

Lindbergh: Thanks, Sergeant. I'm certain Herr Boll will do just fine. If you'll excuse me, Professor ...

(*Michaud starts to leave.*)

Lindbergh: No, don't go, Professor. We can continue our talk while Herr Boll trims the locks.

Don't take too much off. Trim, understand?

Boll: Ya, Ya. Trim. I understand.

(*Boll removes a cloth and equipment from his small bag and begins cutting Lindbergh's hair. O'Neil watches for a moment, then turns to leave.*)

O'Neil: Remember Boll, outside this building.

Boll: Ya! Ya! Outside this building.

Lindbergh: Thanks again, Sergeant.

O'Neil: See you later, Colonel, Professor.

(*O'Neil leaves.*)

Lindbergh: Professor Michaud, I was in the Pacific a few weeks ago and left appalled at the atrocities ... on both sides. Perhaps not to the same degree, but still reprehensible. The Nazis ... the SS ... must be held accountable. But it would be wrong, unjust, to blame all Germans for Hitler's madness. Just as it would be to hold all Americans ... all British ... accountable for wrongs done by our military. None of us can take pride in the bombings ... the destruction of cities and towns ... churches, schools, museums. I came through Munich ... the killing of civilians and children ...

(*While Lindbergh talks, Boll cuts his hair. Michaud stares at the two men, seemingly oblivious to what is being said. The light fades, and a scene is revealed in the back of the stage behind a veil. A group of naked*) *men—some being shaved while an SS guard strikes others. Suddenly, lights up. Michaud screams, grabs a truncheon from the table, and strikes Boll. Lindbergh jumps from the table as O'Neil rushes in and grabs Michaud. Stage darkens.)*

Act Three

Act Three is set in Fuller's office that afternoon. O'Neil is reading a newspaper. Colonel Fuller enters, and O'Neil rises.

O'Neil: Afternoon, Colonel.

Fuller: Sergeant. Has Major Wilder arrived?

O'Neil: Yessir, 'bout an hour ago. I told him about the German ... what happened. He said he'd have a chat with the MPs and come right over with the latest ...

Fuller: How'd you find our battered and bruised barber?

O'Neil: Slightly bruised but hardly battered. The professor's so weak, I was surprised he could even swing the club. Fact is, there's a few added bruises ...

Fuller: Oh! How's that?

O'Neil: Seems our German barber gave the medics a hard time when they tried to examine him, so they called in a couple of MPs. Those suspicious guys decided to look under his left arm ...

Fuller: ... And found a tattoo? Blood type? SS?

O'Neil: Yep .. Yes, sir.

Fuller: One of Dora's finest?

O'Neil: No, sir. At least the MPs don't think so. The Kraut says he was with the Waffen SS fighting the Russkies near Prague. When he heard Hitler was kaput, he decided he'd rather be on our side of the line ... said Ivan was ... (*Smiles*) kinda hard on SS types.

Fuller: I can't understand why he'd think that. Anyway, we'll let Wilder sort it out. How about Lindbergh?

O'Neil: Seems OK. Came by about forty-five minutes ago. Said he had met Major Wilder and had a nice talk. He and the navy lieutenant are off to check an aircraft line in the next tunnel. Said they could get along on their own, and I showed them a way on a map. Said they'd be leaving for Leipzig but would stop by—if it is convenient.

Fuller: Fine. Does he know the German's SS?

O'Neil: Yessir. I hope that was OK. He was pretty concerned about the guy, so I told him.

Fuller: No problem.

O'Neil: Colonel Fuller, can I speak freely?

Fuller: I thought you always had ...

O'Neil: Yessir ... mostly.

Fuller: Go ahead.

O'Neil: Well, sir. I know Colonel Lindbergh is a great guy ... a real hero, but ... well ... sometimes he's sort of funny ...

Fuller: Funny?

O'Neil: Yes, sir. Says some weird things. Like, he's really worried about the poor Germans. Talked about their starving. On the way from Munich, starving kids along the way. Shit ... sorry, sir. They may be a mite hungry now that they got to share what they got with the poor sons-of-bitches they worked to death. But they were sure fat when we got here. Kids starving ... Heck, they're after chocolate. Whenever they see a GI, they come running. They know we're suckers. I've seen some take the chocolate, then spit at the GI behind his back ...

Fuller: Well, Sergeant, perhaps in time he'll come to understand.

O'Neil: Hope so. It just ain't right. And he kept calling the poor guys in the tunnels workers, never slaves. He also said the ones he saw were dirty but not too badly fed. I almost told him we had buried those that starved or were beaten to death.

Fuller: Maybe the professor can get him to understand. And how is Michaud?

O'Neil: Still sacked out, since at least an hour ago. The medics gave him a shot to calm him down.

Fuller: Good. Let the poor guy sleep. I've a pretty good idea what set him off—losing his hair at Buchenwald. The shrinks call it a flashback. Kinda like seeing a gun that resembles the one that killed your parents. That's from a case we had back in Iowa ...

O'Neil: You mean I'm going to have flashbacks about losing my hair in boot camp?

Fuller: You just might! (*Frowns*) You know, Sergeant, there is a similarity. That GI barber clipped your hair to the tune of "You're in the Army Now." It symbolized a new world ... a new way of life.

O'Neil: It sure was ...

Fuller: And for some ... considering the Depression ... and ... except for combat ... might have been much better.

O'Neil: Yessir ... It sure was. The farm could hardly support Mom and Dad, and jobs in Prairie View were mighty scarce. Guess I was hoping for a new way of life. Not sure I want to be a civilian again, but I guess they won't keep me with this bum leg. Maybe I'll let my hair grow long and go to college. Colonel Fuller, about the SS ... did they really shave a man's balls?

Fuller: According to the professor, every hair on a prisoner's body. It was their way of telling new inmates, "Your ass is our ass. We can do whatever we want." As Michaud put it, it was the first step to destroying a person's humanity ... to reduce the individual to something less than human.

(*They are interrupted by a sound off stage.*)

O'Neil: That's probably Major Wilder.

(*Wilder enters, salutes, and speaks.*)

Wilder: Afternoon, Colonel. I hear I missed quite a show this morning.

Fuller: Ben. (*Smiles*) Yeah ... and I missed the party due to a court-martial. From what the sergeant tells me, our distinguished visitor has something to remember. The Kraut was so startled by Michaud's attack he darn near scalped Lindbergh. Would have been hard to explain to headquarters. You satisfied there was no connection to Dora?

Wilder: Yeah, I'm satisfied. Nothing to connect him to Dora. He lives with his sister, really was a barber before the SS. If he had been at Dora or one of the sub-camps, I don't believe he would have stayed in the vicinity.

Fuller: Makes sense. When you're finished, we'll hand him over to the POW camp in Nordhausen.

O'Neil: Colonel ... 'scuse me. If you can spare me, I'd like to check on the professor ...

Fuller: That's fine, Sergeant. I think just this once I'll declare you sparable.

O'Neil: (*Smiling*) Thank you, sir. Major. (*Leaves*)

Fuller: Well Ben, what's new on your front? O'Neil tells me you had a chance to meet our distinguished visitor.

Wilder: That I did, and it ties in with what I learned at headquarters.

Fuller: Oh! Sounds interesting.

Wilder: It seems our ordnance visitors threw us a curve ... less interested in justice than I was led to believe. Headquarters learned that upwards of fifty of the rockets experts had been captured in Bavaria, in the village of Oberammergau. And get this: they were taken there from here by none other than SS General Hans Kammler!

Fuller: Ha! Our No. 1 bad guy ... Mr. Hyde through and through ...

Wilder: ... who disappeared before our troops moved in. The civilians decided it was time to throw in the towel and contacted a platoon of the Forty Fourth Infantry Division. Within hours, it appears, the Ordnance Special Mission V2 took custody and slammed the door on any contact.

Fuller: On what basis?

Wilder: Top secret. The word is they did not want the Soviets to know who they had. They might use family members in the Soviet zone to draw the rocket experts to their side.

Fuller: Sounds more like an enemy than an ally ...

Wilder: You got it! Rear-echelon types at head-quarters—who now outnumber us—don't think the Krauts are all that bad. A couple of nights ago I overheard a soused major saying we ought to have helped them against the Russians, as though the Red Army hadn't saved American lives.

Fuller: Must work for General Patton. I've heard talk the general's all for taking-on our ex-ally ... not waiting for Ivan to catch his breath.

Wilder: You got it right!. The major was a Third Army staff replacement ... raring to go fight. Behind the lines, of course.

Fuller: You think it is serious, Ben? Or just bullshit talk?

Wilder: Mostly bullshit …. from shoe clerks turned majors who don't want to go home. But the guy claimed he heard Patton say he'd gladly take on von Rundstedt as his chief of staff. (*Frowns*) Seriously, Harry, Patton's not alone. I've heard some generals say we ought to kick the hell out of the communists while we've got the muscle. God knows the Brits are done in—out of money and blood. Truman won't get sucked in. Still, we can't discount the danger. The Russians are real crazies …

Fuller: God, that's scary. I agree with you on Truman. He won't let it happen. Stalin will push for all the territory he can control, but from what I know about Truman, he won't be pushed around … Now, how do you tie in Lindbergh?

Wilder: I met him when I first got back, and we had lunch. Gosh, you can't help but be awed by the guy—world's greatest aviator—but very unpretentious …

Fuller: I can hear it now: What'd you do in the war, Gramps? Met Charles Lindbergh, the great American aviator. Even had lunch with him. Gosh, Gramps, you musta been real important!

Wilder: (*Smiling*) Yeah! I was a bit awestruck. I was all of nine when he crossed the Atlantic. Hero? You bet! I'd have paddled the Atlantic just to see him. I still see him as one of the greatest

Americans in spite of how he was against aiding the Brits in '40 ... '41. And his crack about
the Jews trying to suck us into a war. That sure
rubbed my family the wrong way ... But I suspect he's learned a lot.

Fuller: You implied he might be of some assistance
in your criminal investigations ...

Wilder: We talked about Dora and what Michaud
had told him. He seemed to feel that the professor was exaggerating, but when I laid out a
bunch of facts, he seemed to come around. That,
plus what he has seen here should be enough to
invite his support.

Fuller: In what way?

Wilder: I expressed the view that ordnance was
determined to employ the German rocket experts ... and were not especially concerned as
to whether they were committed Nazis, SS, or
guilty of any war crimes. I went all out stressing
the importance of holding the Germans accountable for what had happened here ... of the death
of some twenty thousand prisoners.

Fuller: And his reaction?

Wilder: (*Smiling*) Well, he didn't disagree. Harry,
I believe he understood ... that it reached his
humanity.

Fuller: But where does the help come into play?

Wilder: Influence. I believe he can reach people in high places in Washington. He may not have been a favorite of Roosevelt's, but I'll bet he can reach many in congress, the military, especially high up in the air corps. I think he can open that closed door at ordnance and let us in to find out exactly what their involvement might have been. I want to know who that SS major was that Michaud heard at Dora and interviewed Garon at Buchenwald. He's got much to answer for ... no doubt about it ...

Fuller: OK. O'Neil tells me Lindbergh is coming by to pay his respects before departing. He's all yours; it'll be interesting to hear his response.

(*O'Neil enters.*)

O'Neil: Sorry, Colonel, Major. I have some bad news: Professor Michaud died.

Wilder: Damn!

Fuller: Details, Sergeant?

O'Neil: The medics said he was sleeping soundly, but when they decided it was time for a little food, they found no pulse. The doc came right away and said he was dead, that his worn out heart just gave up. Doc said he'd be available should you want to talk.

(*Knock on the door.*)

Fuller: Thanks, Sergeant. That's probably Lindbergh. Bid him enter.

(*Lindbergh and Kroeler enter and O'Neil departs.*)

Fuller: (*Standing*) Colonel Lindbergh, I'm sorry I missed you when you arrived.

Lindbergh: Colonel Fuller. (*Lindbergh and Fuller shake hands.*) Sergeant O'Neil served as a perfect host and tour guide. Colonel, Lieutenant Kroeler ...

Fuller: Lieutenant. (*Fuller and Kroeler shake hands, and Fuller turns back to Lindbergh.*) I understand you have met Major Wilder.

Lindbergh: Yes, we had a nice chat at lunch. And Major, I've thought much about what you said ...

Fuller: Colonel, I'm afraid I have some bad news. I understand you met Professor Michaud ... We just learned that the professor has died ... heart attack.

Lindbergh: I'm sorry to hear that. We had a long discussion, and I learned how horrible conditions were. I also talked to one of the workers who said some 25,000 died ... I suspect that was grossly exaggerated ...

Wilder: Not much. From the German records, our figure is 20,000 who died from malnutrition, beatings, disease, overwork, and executions. Yes,

Colonel, a real hell on earth, and we need your help.

Lindbergh: (*Frowning*) Help? I suppose you're speaking as a war crimes investigator?

Wilder: Exactly. You know what happened here, and your influence and contacts in Washington can help in bringing the guilty to an accounting. The ordnance corps—Ordnance Special Mission V2—has a large number of civilian rocket experts in custody and is holding them incommunicado. We are determined to open that door and interrogate the lot.

Lindbergh: You have my understanding and sympathy, but I doubt you can find a worse advocate. I'm not in good standing with the American public, nor with the government in Washington, nor with the army. Back in the thirties, I sought army support for Dr. Robert Goddard, our leading rocket expert, to no avail. Had we placed as much into rocket development as the Germans, I'm convinced the Nazis would have been relegated to second place.

Wilder: How do you explain the military's indifference?

Lindbergh: The cost, plus the fact that during the Depression we were not gearing up for war ... Hitler was. With the outbreak of war in 1939, we did begin to build up our forces, but rockets were—wisely, I believe—passed over in favor of heavy bombers—B-17s, B-24s—as the best offensive weapons. And consider this: had the Nazis put the resources devoted to ballistic rockets into the production of jet fighters such as the twin-engine Me-262, the course of the war would have been quite different.

Wilder: How's that?

Lindbergh: Several squadrons of jet fighters would have affected the outcome of the Battle of Britain in 1940. But even if they did not enter combat until later, the Allied strategic bombing campaign might have proved much too costly to continue. And in 1944, the invasion of Normandy would have been problematic without air superiority. (*Smiles*) All in all, I'd say Hitler's decision to pour resources into rockets while ignoring the value of jet fighters was in the Allies' favor.

Wilder: Reading between the lines, I sense you're saying that the German rocket experts actually have little to offer.

Lindbergh: We led Germany in the science of rocketry. I feel the German software, especially the test results, offer much value. The Germans, having worked out the engineering bugs, can save us time and money in producing our own ballistic long-range rockets.

Wilder: (*Smiling*) If we have the rockets and the test results, then ordnance has a weak argument for keeping the Germans.

Lindbergh: If army ordnance needs a reason, I'd say it would be to keep them out of the hands of the communists. Considering the state of Germany, my guess is they'd throw their lot in with whatever country offered room and board ...

Wilder: At the risk of revealing a mean streak, I'd keep them away from the Soviets by locking 'em up and throwing away the key. I guess what it adds up to is "we use 'em or lose 'em." That's hard to accept ... that some will escape justice, even, as you suggest, they were doing us a favor in taking their Führer down the wrong path. (*He turns to Fuller.*) Harry, you've been rather quiet. I sense you've taken off your uniform and returned to the bench.

Fuller: (*Smiling*) Am I that easy to read? I plead guilty—once a judge, always a judge.

Lindbergh: Mind sharing your thoughts, Judge Fuller?

Fuller: Well, if I were hearing the case, I would have to decide if facts tilt towards assigning the Germans to ordnance to exploit or Major Wilder and his people to investigate. And, if the facts establish a case, prosecute. It's a case of ambiguities. The end result is obscure. When mom and dad split, who gets the child to provide the best future?

Lindbergh: Ah, yes. War produces ambiguities, as does peace.

Fuller: Exactly. I know where Major Wilder stands. How about you? Do you favor exploiting the Germans under the "use them or lose them" argument?

Lindbergh: Once I was convinced that aviation was certain to advance the welfare of peoples of all nations. I still believe that. But what can be used in peace can be applied to war. Today, we see about us the horrible impact of air power. But it's not difficult to see rockets beyond the V2 able to reach any target on earth. Yet, rockets without warheads have even greater potential—the ability to lift satellites into orbit. "Control the high ground" is fundamental to battle. It sold aircraft for observation in World War One. What rockets can accomplish is limited only by one's imagination—and resources. The Nazis ... the Soviets ... the US ... other nations with human and financial resources can produce rockets that can reach to any place on earth without warning— and do it soon. We must be in the forefront.

Wilder: Then, I gather, you are on the side of using them.

Lindbergh: We teamed up with the communists to defeat the Nazis. But their values are not our values. Even in peace, the world's only two powerful nations are in conflict. But our goal must be to avoid military conflict. As a president said a half century ago, we need to speak softly but carry a bit stick. Back when the war began, I argued that we best stay out and that England ought to reach an arrangement with Germany ...

Wilder: Cut a deal with Hitler!

Lindbergh: Germany was the one country strong enough to stand up to the Soviet Union. I believed that in 1939, and I believe Germany stands as the best defense the West has today.

Wilder: That defense, I gather, includes rockets assisted by Germans, even Nazis. (*Smiles*) Well, that may be true—I'm no diplomat or military strategist—but I would like to pluck out those that bloodied their hands here at Dora. If we don't hang the guilty, we might even give them back to ordnance on parole from prison.

Fuller: Ben, you sound like you might make a pretty good judge.

Lindbergh: (*Smiling*) On this, I think we can agree. Thank you, gentlemen. And now, Lieutenant Kroeler and I best be on our way to Leipzig. And please convey my thanks again to Sergeant O'Neil. He was a first-class guide.

(*The three shake hands. Lindbergh and Kroeler depart. Fuller and Wilder sit down after a pause.*)

Fuller: Well, Ben. It would seem you are left running down lowly SS guards. Landing little fish while the big ones swim away.

Wilder: Perhaps, perhaps not. Lately I've been toying with the idea of running for congress when I turn in this uniform. When I sensed the way Lindbergh was headed—use them or lose them—I knew I would take that road. A great platform to prod the US Army and the top German rocket engineers to acknowledge what happened here—a first step to seeing justice done for the thousands who died and thousands more who suffered.

Fuller: (*Smiling*) Sorry that I'll not be registered in your congressional district. You'd have my support and vote.

Wilder: (*Smiling*) I'll have my campaign fundraiser get in touch. (*Frowns*) If Michaud ever looks down from on high, I only hope someday he sees an assembly of German rocket engineers in the dock, especially one known to occasionally wear the uniform of an SS major.

Fuller: Now Ben, let's attempt to locate the ubiquitous Sergeant O'Neil. I'd like to surprise him with the order I just received sending him stateside. But I know darn well he probably knew of the order even before it was printed.

Wilder: (*Laughing*) You know, Harry, when I reach Congress, I just might make O'Neil my chief of staff. The two of us might even have an impact on Washington.

(*The curtain falls.*)

Afterword

The play, though fiction, follows the facts and chronology of the American exploitation of German technology and technologists following the end of the European conflict and the beginning of the Cold War. The late Dr. Wernher von Braun is only hinted at in the play, which takes place in 1945, and, at that time, unconnected to the war crimes involved in the Nazi V2 rocket program. War crimes investigators are eager to discover who might be directly connected to the underground rocket facility and the use of slave labor. In later years, that connection is made leading to the following observation by Professor Carl Sagan of Cornell University: *I found many things disturbing about von Braun's career—his willingness to work for the Wehrmacht and the SS, to accept a commission in the SS ... and to use slave labor in the production of the V2s.*

Some names in the play have been changed, though not Charles Lindbergh. The reason is that Lindbergh documented in his *Wartime Journal* his visit to Camp Dora and Mittelwerk of June 10, 1945, as a member of the US Navy Technical Mission. What is said in the play follows what he wrote.

Many may wonder how Wernher von Braun and upwards of one hundred members of his German rocket team could escape accountability for their services to Nazi Germany—some as ardent Nazis, others as commissioned officers in the notorious SS; even war criminals as defined at the war crimes trial at Nuremberg. The answer, we belatedly have learned, was through the dedication of the US government, both military and civilian, to scrub or hide the truth. But as one of today's German leaders declared when a celebration honoring Dr. von Braun was canceled due to his Nazi connection and use of slave labor, "You cannot isolate technology from history."

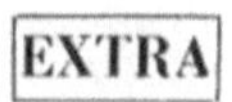

PARIS EDITION

EXTRA **THE STARS AND STRIPES** **EXTRA**

Daily Newspaper of U.S. Armed Forces in the European Theater of Operations

Vol. 1—No. 279   1 Fr.   1 Fr.   Wednesday, May 2, 1945

HITLER DEAD

Fuehrer Fell at CP, German Radio Says; Doenitz at Helm, Vows War Will Continue

Churchill Hints Peace Is at Hand

Sources

1945. *Spearhead in the West, 1941–1945, US Third Armored Division.* Liberated the Dora concentration camp and discovered the underground V2 rocket plant.

1945, April 17. *Stars and Stripes,* "Tunnels of Hell: 22,000 Nazi Slaves Made V2s In Deep Underground Factory." The US Army's newspaper that covered the Third Armored Division at Dora and the underground factory.

1947. *United States of America v. Kurt Andrae, et al.,* National Archives Microfilm M1079. (Not released until 1981.) A follow-on to the Nuremberg trials, only minor persons were tried and convicted. von Braun was "invited" to testify, but his employer, the US Army, refused to make him available.

1958. V2 by General Walter Dornberger. The author organized and directed the German rocket program. Though self-serving, the book provides excellent details and insight into the German effort, including the conflict between the Wehrmacht and the SS to control the rocket program after Hitler expressed interest. It is significant that the author never mentions the use of slave labor.

1964. *Crossbow and Overcast* by James McGovern. Excellent details about the effort by the British to destroy the V1 and V2 operations.

1966. "Freedom of Information Act," signed into law by President Lyndon Johnson. (Public Law 89-554 as amended in 1986, 2002, 2007.)

1968. *Doctors of Mercy* (Chapter 28) and *Witches of God* (Chapter 13) by Christian Bernadac. (Details of Dora and the underground rocket factory from testimony provided by French survivors). Published in Paris by France-Empire Press.

1970. *The Wartime Journals of Charles A. Lindbergh* by Charles A. Lindbergh Jr. The entry of June 10, 1945. Decidedly pro-German, he documented his moral outrage at the conditions of the underground rocket plant but preferred not to connect this to von Braun or other members of his German rocket team.

1975. *Project Paperclip: German Scientists and the Cold War* by Clarence G. Lasby. Though hampered by military secrecy and non-cooperation, the author has compiled an excellent first study of the American exploitation of Germans at the end of WWII.

1975. *Dora: The Nazi Concentration Camp Where Modern Space Technology Was Born* by Jean Michael. (First published in US in 1979.) No person of conscience can read this account without praying that justice be rendered. And it was, on a limited basis. It led to one of Wernher von Braun's key aides to renounce his US citizenship in 1983 rather than face trial and being revealed as a war criminal.

1978. *Hitler's Last Weapons: The Underground War Against the V1 and V2* by Jozef Garlinski. A well-researched account by a WWII Polish officer who worked in the underground rocket plant, then survived Auschwitz. Excellent account of the testing of V2 rockets in Poland.

1979. *The Rocket Team* by Frederick I. Ordway III and Michell R. Sharp. This is a well-researched and well-documented history of the German rocket program but glosses over the wartime role of the Germans involved in such crimes as the use of slave labor.

1979. The Justice Department established the Office of Special Investigations (OSI) to track down Nazi war criminals.

1981. US National Archives made available transcripts of the 1947 Dora-Nordhausen War Crimes Trials.

1982. *The Pledge Betrayed: America and Britain and the Denazification of Post-War Germany* by Thomas M. Bower. Goes beyond the German V2 effort and the role of the Germans involved but is of considerable value in learning of the effort to utilize former Nazis in reacting to the Cold War.

1987. "The Nazi Connection." A *Frontline* report on PBS. Report by Tom Bower of the British Broadcasting System (BBS). Also, *The Paperclip Conspiracy: The Hunt For Nazi Scientists* by Tom Bower.

1990. *Science, Technology, and Reparations: Exploitation and Plunder in Postwar Germany* by John Gimbel. A carefully researched and documented study that concludes that the employment of "ardent Nazis" in the exploitation effort was not a "conspiracy" to subvert national policy but a conscious decision by government officials up to and including the president.

1995. *The Rocket and the Reich: Peenemunde and the Coming of the Ballistic Missile Era* by Michael J. Neufeld. A curator of WWII history at the National Air and Space Museum, Dr. Neufeld has produced the best documented history of the Nazi rocket program, including the dark sides of the effort.

1995. *The Nazi Racketeers: Dreams of Space and Crimes of War* by Dennis Piszkiewicz. The author is a post-WWII space enthusiast enthralled with the history of the German program, especially the Nazi connection and the use of slave labor.

1996. *The Peenemunde Wind Tunnels: A Memoir* by
Peter P. Wegener. Wegener was a young Luftwaffe officer assigned to the supersonic wind
tunnels of the German rocket program. It is of
interest in that he was sent to the underground
factory at the end of the war and was appalled by
what he saw. Later, he declined to join Dr. von
Braun in the US but accepted employment with
the US Navy. He is a retired professor from Yale
University.

1997. *Planet Dora: A Memoir of the Holocaust and the
Birth of the Space Age* by Yves Beon (with an
introduction by Michael Neufeld). Beon writes:
"In a very real sense, the greatest technological
achievement of the twentieth century had its
origins in the enslavement and murder of thousands of innocent people, the downpayment of a
Faustian bargain that still tarnishes our reach for
the stars."

1998. *Wernher von Braun: The Man who Sold the
Moon*, another contribution by Dennis Piszkiewicz. Well-written and exceptionally well-
documented. He concludes that Wernher von
Braun willingly joined the Nazi cause and was
an accomplice in its crimes in order to build
rockets. He sold his soul to reach that goal.

1998, October 8. The president signed "Public
Law 105-246: The Nazi War Crimes Disclosure
Act." The Act established the Nazi War Crimes

Interagency Working Group (IAG) to locate, inventory, recommend for declassification, and make available to the public all classified Nazi war criminal records, subject to certain specified exceptions. Reports of the IAG can be found on archives.gov

1998 (France), 2003 (US). *A History of the Dora Camp: The Story of the Nazi Slave Labor Camp That Secretly Manufactured V-2 Rockets* by Andre Sellier (with a forward by Michael J. Neufeld). An extensive and well-documented horror story of Dora-Mittelbau, one of the Nazi's largest concentration camps devoted to slave laborers assigned to the underground V2 rocket factory.

1999. *Power to Explore: A History of Marshall Space Flight Center, 1960-1990* by Andrew J. Dunar and Stephen P. Waring. In due course, even the government that employed the German rocket experts (and heaped them with honors) has been moved to accept the truth of their services to Nazi Germany.

2003. *Rocket Man: Robert H. Goddard and the Birth of the Space Age* by David A. Clary. A commendable biography of America's pioneering rocket scientist. Especially interesting is his widow's long battle to achieve recognition for her late husband and compensation from the government over use of his patents.

2007. *von Braun: Dreamer of Space/Engineer of War* by Michael J. Neufeld. More detailed than Piszkiewicz's biography but arrives at the same conclusion. It was Neufeld that discovered documents unavailable for half a century that directly connected von Braun in his own words to the Nazi slave labor program.

Uncle Edgar's Secret List

A Radio Play
approximately 30 minutes

The Set

A stage in a radio station. Josh and Emilie sit at a table with microphones. The announcer is at a lectern with a microphone to share with the archivist and bartender. A large sign demands,

"SILENCE: ON THE AIR"

The Cast

The Announcer: male or female, with a strong voice

Josh Pedersen: male in mid-twenties

Emilie Robinette: female, about eighty

Archivist: middle-aged male

Barmaid: a no-nonsense female

The Play

Opens with music playing that fades as the announcer talks.

Announcer: Welcome to *Satin Soap's Midnight Mysteries.* Satin Soap, so soft and silky that even new-born babies cry for a bath. Tonight we open our new season with "Uncle Edgar's Secret List," a thrilling tale that takes place in our nation's capital. It involves Josh Pedersen, a young graduate student doing research at the Library of Congress who encounters a most remarkable lady, one who involves him in an escapade that reveals a Draconian threat to our national security. Now, mystery fans, relax with your caffeine-free beverage and no-salt pretzels and thrill to "Uncle Edgar's Secret List."

❧ Music, to set the tone ❧

Josh: Arriving in Washington to complete research for my doctorate, I had two immediate tasks to complete. The first was to arrange for a study desk at the Library of Congress, something easily accomplished. And the second, to find a place to live, a task aided by the library with a FOR RENT section on a bulletin board. This, I discovered, would lead to an encounter with a most remarkable woman, one who would expose me to knowledge that if made public would shatter the very foundation of our republic. I shudder as I recall the experience.

❧ *Music* ❧

Josh: Hello. I'm calling about the apartment you have available.

Emilie: Yes. Where are you calling from?

Josh: The Library of Congress

Emilie: That figures. It's the only place I list. Why are you there?

Josh: I'm a doctoral student and came to apply for a study desk.

Emilie: Good! You'll need one if you expect to get anything accomplished. You have the address. Walk east on Pennsylvania Avenue. When you reach Third Street, go left ... that's north. Mid-block you'll find the address ... A row house. Climb the iron steps and ring the bell. Wait. I'll get there.

Josh: I followed her instructions and found it less than a fifteen-minute walk. As I climbed the steps to the front door, I noticed an entrance to the basement, A common sight among the row houses. The private entrance to the apartment, I reasoned. Several seconds after ringing the door bell, the door opened slightly, and someone peeked out. I called about the apartment, I said. Words meant to place the person at ease.

Emilie: Yes, of course.

Josh: The door opened to reveal a slight, elderly woman.

Emilie: Come in, young man. And we'll have a nice talk, and you can tell me all about yourself.

Josh: The door opened wide into the hallway. She stood about five feet tall but slightly stooped, indicating she had probable shrunken a couple of inches. Her hair was iron gray, cut rather short. She led me into the parlor off to the right. A quick glance suggested it had been decorated in the 1920s with nothing changed.

I'm afraid you'll be bored by my story, I remarked as she invited me to sit on the sofa and took a chair facing me.

Emilie: I doubt it. We all have interesting stories to tell ... unless something is best kept secret. That's up to you.

Josh: Thank you. Well, Mrs. ...

Emilie: Miss ... Robinette

Josh: Miss Robinette, I'm Jonathan, better known as Josh, Pedersen. I was raised in the small town of Macon in north central Missouri. Dad was a veterinarian, mom taught in middle school. I received my BS in political science at Westminster—that's in Fulton, where Churchill gave his famous iron-curtain speech ...

Emilie: (*Interrupting*) I'm quite aware of that young man, I am very well informed. Go on.

Josh: MA from the University of Missouri. Now pursuing a doctorate.

Emilie: In political science, I suppose. What is the subject of your research?

Josh: The impact of the House Un-American Activities Committee on the Foreign Service. There was a long pause, as if she was dwelling on how to respond, then changed the subject.

Emilie: Well, young man. I believe you'll do quite well. Come look at where you'll be staying.

Josh: She led me to the basement, which I found perfect for my needs. A private bath. A small bed and comfortable chair with a good reading light in the living area, along with a desk and chair. Also a counter holding a toaster oven, with a small refrigerator beneath. What she asked as rent was within my budget.

Emilie: Are you prepared to move in?

Josh: Tomorrow, I responded enthusiastically. I'll stay tonight in the motel and come over in the morning. I have little to move ... a few books and even fewer clothes. Is it safe to park on the street?

Emilie: Quite safe. The street is well lit. Parking should offer no problem.

Josh: She led me out and smiled as we shook hands. I literally danced as I departed.

~❧ Music ❧~

Josh: I settled in quite easily. She was so quiet I hardly knew she was above me. Coming back from the library on my second Friday, I found a note on my door inviting me to join her for tea. I was pleased to accept. When she opened the door, I received a pleasant greeting.

Emilie: Good afternoon, Josh.

Josh: Good afternoon, Miss Robinette.

Emilie: I prefer to be called Miss Emilie.

Josh: I stand corrected, Miss Emilie.

We had a light-hearted conversation as she described some of the characters who had inhabited her neighborhood known as Capitol Hill. Then I inquired, Miss Emilie, did you work at the Library of Congress?

Emilie: No, Josh. I had that in mind when I studied history, but it was not to be. After getting an undergraduate degree at George Washington University, I went on to earn a master's at Georgetown. That produced an offer from the US National Archives, where I spent nearly forty years. It was most satisfying. When you get around to doing research there, you will find it both productive and interesting. Most of the archivists I worked with are gone, but there are one or two I want you to meet. They can be of much help in your research.

Josh: Thank you, Miss Emilie. This is something I look forward to.

~⊛~ Music ~⊛~

Josh: The following Friday produced another invitation for tea that included a plate of Walker's shortbread. As soon as we were seated and tea was served, she asked …

Emilie: Well, Josh, what do you think of the library?

Josh: I delayed responding long enough to flash back to my first visit to the main reading room, then declared: beautiful, irreplaceable, a national treasure. I had five days working in the main reading room before being assigned a study desk in the stacks. That left an impression I'll always remember.

Emilie: Well put, young man ... And added to the beauty of the place, it has one of the world's best collections of the printed word.

Josh: As well as a growing collection of photography and film, I was told. And I bet you, being so close, you've spent many an hour there.

Emilie: Indeed I have. As a child I lived some distance, but on an occasional weekend I would come to stay with my grandmother and my uncle Edgar. They lived but a few blocks from here. Uncle Edgar would take me to the library. He knew every nook and cranny

Josh: Did your uncle work there?

Emilie: Yes, but only part time while at university. He did have a major role in creating the library catalogue system ...

Josh: She was obviously proud of the connection.

Emilie: And let me warn you, Josh, don't get so carried away by your research that you'll forget that the library closes at ten. One young man who stayed here in the apartment failed to hear the warning bell. Suddenly the lights went out, and it took nearly two hours to find his way out.

Josh: She obviously enjoyed telling the story, as I enjoyed hearing it.

❧ Music ❧

Josh: I would learn much more about Uncle Edgar in the weeks ahead. Friday tea was a given and even expanded to accompanying Miss Emilie to a nearby church on Sunday. I looked forward to our visits and soon discovered that Miss Emilie needed me. Her eyesight was very poor, and she had given up reading, instead depending on television and radio to keep informed. One afternoon, while I was alone while she prepared tea, I wandered about the room. Suddenly, several photographs on the mantel struck me like a thunderbolt. J. Edgar Hoover! Uncle Edgar … the late Uncle Edgar was the FBI director! Had I known more of his early life, I would have suspected. She entered the room and observed me staring at the photographs.

Emilie: Yes, that's a young Uncle Edgar, the long-time director of the FBI. I hope your knowing this doesn't affect our relationship. He has become very controversial.

Josh: No, no. Not at all, I insisted. I had read of the secret files Hoover was said to have kept on many influential people, including several presidents, and wondered what she might know. Were you very close?

Emilie: No … not following my grandmother Anne's death in 1938. Ann was his mother. He moved some distance away, and a few years later, following my parents' death, I inherited this house. He would telephone occasionally, but I saw him only once shortly before he died.

Josh: I didn't quite know what to say and had a feeling she had more to add. I was right.

Emilie: Of course you know he kept secret files ...

Josh: Yes, I had read that. I had also read that he used what was in those files as leverage to maintain and enhance his power.

Emilie: I'm not one to defend what he may or may not have done. But I do know that he always acted in what he believed to be in America's best interests.

Josh: Her tone suggested self-doubt. Yes, I suppose even many who were critical granted that.

Emilie: Perhaps. Now Josh ...

Josh: She paused a few moments, then continued.

Emilie: I have in mind enlisting you in what I am convinced may be best for the country ...

Josh: Well ... I was about to beg off, being concerned it might impact my research.

Emilie: Hear what I have to say ... Give it careful consideration. If you want no part, I'll understand

Josh: Fair enough. My reply drew a satisfied smile.

Emilie: Good! Yes, Uncle Edgar did maintain many secret files. But most were destroyed by his secretary following his death in 1972, as he had instructed. But not all. Several weeks before he died, he came here on an unexpected visit. He looked poorly ,and I thought he might not last much longer. He had a package, six very important files, he insisted, that must, in due course, be available to a certain historian. But not for at least a decade following his death. I believe he had concluded I was the one person he could trust.

Josh: But Miss Emilie, I understood he was very close to his assistant director.

Emilie: Yes, Clyde Tolson. But Tolson was in very poor health. Besides, Uncle Edgar had a special responsibility placed on Clyde.

Josh: My reaction was one of increased interest, and I leaned forward so as to not miss a word

Emilie: From what I understood, my uncle was very concerned with the direction the Nixon administration was taking. If Edgar did not survive Nixon's presidency, which of course he did not, Mr. Tolson was to deliver a file to me that was to be kept in secret with the other files. As I am now telling you, I did exactly as he asked.

Josh: You have these files here? In this house? This produced a smile.

Emilie: No, young man. They have been secluded in a far more secure place. They are filed in the National Archives!

Josh: Her answer jolted me. But, but, Miss Emilie, this makes them available to anyone ... does it not? She left the room for a brief period then returned with a single sheet of paper.

Emilie: At the time I received the files, I was still at the National Archives. There are many old files no longer of interest to anyone. I selected at random seven personnel files of individuals who had worked for the government at least fifty years ago ... no one of any known importance. Each of the files handed to me were secluded under someone else's name. This list has that name and the file I added. In the course of your research, you simply request the files of the names listed ... one of which was provided me by Clyde Tolson.

Josh: Do you know what those files contain?

Emilie: I do not. I made that decision when they came into my possession. I leave the contents to you ... if you decide to play the game.

Josh: She smiled, and I returned the smile, though a bit strained, while thinking: Some game, Miss Emilie! A game of Russian roulette? Could be!

❧ *Music* ❧

Josh: Emilie never offered me the list. The files were never mentioned again, though I understood I was to give her my decision before my stay in Washington ended. My interest increased as the weeks went by. Thus, when I entered the final month of my Washington stay, I gulped a sip of tea during a visit and declared ... Miss Emilie, I'll play the game! I had the intriguing list in my hand within minutes.

❧ Music ❧

Josh: I had become a regular presence in the National Archives and an acknowledged friend of Miss Emilie, as she was known by her colleagues. I was allotted a small cubicle, providing considerable privacy and given what I surmised was extra special assistance. I requested the files from the friendly archivist.

Archivist: No problem, though they must be brought from our retired record's depository some distance away.

Josh: They were on my desk when I arrived the next morning. I took my time scanning the six files provided to Emilie by Uncle Edgar. They covered Presidents Roosevelt—nothing of Truman!—Eisenhower, Kennedy, and Johnson, plus Eleanor Roosevelt and Robert Kennedy. I quickly concluded that the bits and pieces of gossip and fact were nothing that had not already surfaced over the years. I would carry out Hoover's instruction to release the files to a named presidential scholar. I intended to accomplish this by anonymously informing him where they could be found. What he did or did not enter into the historical record was his decision.

❧ Music ❧

Josh: After deciding to play Miss Emilie's "game," but before letting her know, I learned what I could about Director Hoover's assistant, Clyde Tolson—the person responsible for the seventh file delivered to Emilie. The instruction, you may recall, was that she was to receive the file "after Mr. Nixon left office." Richard Nixon resigned the presidency effective August 9, 1974, and the file came to Emilie a week later. Mission accomplished by Mr. Hoover's dedicated aide and companion, who died the next year.

❧ Music ❧

Josh: When I opened the seventh file and realized what it contained, my blood pressure and interest soared. It contained several pages of transcripts of recorded conversations in the Oval Office between President Nixon and his key aide Robert Haldeman. Nixon, who was taping his own conversations, was at the same time being recorded by someone else. The country's leading bugger was being bugged!

There were so few pages of the transcripts that it was evident that the file had been purged by Tolson. This indicated that what remained had to be especially important, at least important to Mr. Tolson. And I immediately understood exactly what had been transcribed: that notorious eighteen and a half minutes missing from a recorded Oval Office conversation! And now, I, Josh Pederson, must be the only person alive who knows exactly what had been erased. And how, if ever revealed, would destroy the very foundation of our self-governing democracy.

Badly shaken, I instinctively knew I must destroy the transcript. Tearing each page into small pieces, I mixed the result, then divided the pile into two parts. Removing my right shoe, I packed the pieces of one pile into the bottom, then did the same for the left shoe. It was a tight fit, but I found I could manage. Replacing the files into their envelopes, I took them to the archivist at the end of the hall, explaining they were no longer needed and could be returned to the depository. I thanked him for his assistance as I departed. He asked that I pass on his kind regards to Miss Emilie.

I left the archives building at the Pennsylvania Avenue entrance, crossed the street, and walked in the direction of the White House. At the first trash receptacle, I removed my right shoe and shook out the bits of paper. A block further on, I did the same with the left. Feeling relieved, I glanced around, only to discover I was directly in front of the J. Edgar Hoover Building. Could I, might I ... have been observed? And can this formidable institution put together those bits of paper? This attack of paranoia was brought under control in the nearest bar. A double scotch, please.

Bartender: Single malt or blend?

Josh: Single malt. Better still, make that a double.

My second shot would be a toast to Miss Emilie, a grand old lady, a dedicated public servant and a true patriot. My hand shook badly as I downed the first scotch. Then I noticed two men had joined me at the bar, one on each side. They wore fedoras, white shirts with dark ties. As my shaking increased, I gulped the second double scotch, holding it with both hands. Suddenly the room began rotating as I toppled from the bar stool. Through a fog, I saw men wearing fedoras bending over me, and in the distance, someone yelled to call 9-1-1. Everything went blank. Then, slowly coming into focus, was Miss Emilie's smiling face and I could hear her say...

Emilie: Well done, Josh!

❧ *Music* ❧

Announcer: Watch your local listing for the next thrilling episode of *Midnight Mysteries* brought to you by Satin Soap, so smooth and soft that even newborn babies cry for a bath.

⤳ Music, ending in a loud note ⤲

The End

The Carolina Meadows PlayReaders Present

a WORLD PREMIERE of

"I'll get the check…"

A (PROBABLY TRUE)
POLITICAL FABLE
IN ONE ACT
BY
ROBERT HUDDLESTON
THURSDAY, MARCH 10
CLUB CENTER AUDITORIUM
7:30 P.M.

CLOSED

CO   G A FRIEND

Ou   invite you to join them for
light   …ents following the performance.

- NO R.S.V.P. -

I'll Get the Check

*A (Probably True) Political Fable
in One Act*

Stage Play Script
*Presented in the Carolina Meadows auditorium
on March 10, 2005*

Preface

On October 10, 1973, Spiro "Ted" Agnew resigned as vice president of the United States during the second term of President Richard Nixon. Agnew's letter of resignation was forwarded to the

National Archives through Secretary of State
Henry Kissinger, but only a copy arrived and
the original letter was never found. In the play, a
federal career archivist in the Bureau of Significant
Documents (BuSig) stands convinced that a former
political aide in the bureau had purloined this
important historical document. When the suspect,
who had been appointed to a high post in the Reagan administration, invites the archivist to lunch, a
plan is set in motion.

> October 10, 1973
>
> To: Honorable Henry A. Kissinger
> US Secretary of State
> Washington DC 20520
>
> Dear Mr. Secretary:
>
> I hereby resign the Office of Vice
> President of the United States,
> effective immediately.
>
> Sincerely,
> *Spiro T. Agnew*

Cast

These characters, listed in order of their appearance, do not represent any person, in or out of jail, living or otherwise. The well-known persons mentioned but not seen can be judged as you will.

Miss Overreach: A prim and proper lady of undetermined age.

Homer Bigelow: Late fifties, slightly balding, and a bit overweight. Rumpled appearance.

Bradley Foster Wheeler III: Mid-forties. Ivy league in manner and dress. Nice personality when sober, but always hustling.

Maurice (a k a "Morris" and "Morry"): Ageless. A Washington native and consummate cynic.

Monica: A young women of solid construction.

G. Dudley Liverpool: A man in his sixties wearing a dirty trenchcoat.

(*Off or on stage*)

Senator Scottsdale: A portly gentleman.

A pair of bimbos: Whatever!

Scene One

The stage is dark. To the left of stage, a spot slowly reveals a man seated at a desk. He picks up the telephone and dials. As the phone rings, a spot to the immediate right of center stage slowly reveals a women at a desk. She answers the telephone.

Miss Overreach: Department of Corporate Entitlements, Undersecretary Wheeler's office. How may I help you?

Bigelow: Mr. Wheeler, please.

Overreach: May I know who's calling?

Bigelow: Homer Bigelow, Bureau of Significant Documents.

Overreach: I'm afraid the undersecretary is quite busy, Mr. Bigelow. Perhaps I might assist you.

Bigelow: No, it's rather personal.

Overreach: (*Curtly*) Does the undersecretary know you, Mr. Bigelow?

Bigelow: Yes.

Overreach: Thank you. I'll see if the undersecretary is available.

(*Overreach presses a buzzer. A spot on the far right of stage slowly reveals a man, feet on desk, reading the* Wall Street Journal. *He presses a button and speaks.*)

Bradley Foster Wheeler, III: Yes, what is it?

Overreach: I'm terribly sorry to bother you, Mr. Wheeler, but a Mr. Bigelow is on line one and he insists he must talk to you.

Wheeler: Bigelow?

Overreach: Yes, a Mr. Homer Bigelow, Bureau of …

Wheeler: (*Interrupting*) Homer! Put him on.

Overreach: Yes sir. Thank you, sir. (*Presses a button on the telephone*) Mr. Bigelow, the undersecretary is on the line.

Bigelow: Thank you. Brad?

Wheeler: Homer! How the hell are you, old buddy?

Bigelow: Great, Brad. And how is the Undersecretary of Corporate Entitlements?

Wheeler: Busy! Busy as hell, Homer. Tough go, but the president looks to me …

Bigelow: I know how busy you are, Brad. But I just wanted you to know that I'm finally "hanging 'em up" … retiring. Last day today. Be in town a while and thought we might have lunch when you can get away …

Wheeler: Homer, that's great news. BuSig can't do without old Homer. But you're due. What's it to be? Golf or fishing?

Bigelow: (*Laughs*) Just one last project to finish and then ... shoes off, beer and popcorn, and nothing but old movies.

Wheeler: Boy, does that sound inviting ... old movies ... popcorn and beer ... About lunch, I just learned my lunch appointment had to butt out. Seems he was summoned to a senate hearing at the last minute. Can you make it today? ... On me, of course ...

Bigelow: I sure can. Whenever and wherever you say.

Wheeler: That's great, old buddy. Can you make the Maison Rouge at one? Reservations all set.

Bigelow: Sure ... I can make it. All duties ended yesterday.

Wheeler: Great! And relax, Homer. (*Laughs*) 'Cuz I'll get the check—to treat my retired old buddy. See ya at one.

(*Light fades on Wheeler. Bigelow hangs up, pauses, picks up the phone and dials.*)

Bigelow: Hello. Agent Lewis, please. (*Pause*) Monica ... Homer Bigelow. It's on sooner than we expected. Can you be ready at one today at the Maison Rouge? (*Pause*) Great! If all goes well, we just may bag our No. 1 suspect.

(*Light fades.*)

Scene Two

Wheeler: (*Scanning about*) Say, there's Jim Baker from the White House. I've got to see him for a moment. Go ahead, Homer. Maurice will take care of you. He's all yours, Maurice. And order me a Wheeler Special.

(*Wheeler disappears behind the potted plants.*)

Bigelow: Morris! How the hell are you? You're looking great!

(*They enthusiastically shake hands.*)

Maurice: Homer! It's great to see you! You been staying out of trouble down the avenue?

Bigelow: Never! Nothing's been right since the demise of Morry's Chili Parlor in favor of Hoover's shrine. Up Morry's, down the FBI bunker ... Hey, old buddy, what's with this "Maurice" bit?

Maurice: Class, Homer, strictly class. My Iranian boss says it fits with the French cuisine. Our French patrons see it as a joke. Say, Homer, is this Wheeler character really a friend?

Bigelow: Well ... to be honest, he's more an old business associate. During the Nixon years he spent some time in BuSig.

Maurice: Good! Play 'em close, Homer. The guy's a class "A" hustler, if you know what I mean. Come's here two, three times a week since Reagan came in and made him an undersecretary. He's yet to pick up his first tab ...

Bigelow: Today he loses his virginity; lunch is his treat.

Maurice: Don't make book on it. He'll keep his cherry until he leaves Uncle Sam and lands a big expense account. I've known him to wait over two hours for one of his pigeons ... a lobbyist coming in from New York .. got stuck in a fog over National. Better check your wallet, Homer. This ain't no chili-dog joint. (*Laughs*)

Bigelow: (*Smiles*) We'll see ...

(*They move to a table at center stage. Bigelow takes a seat as Maurice snaps his fingers. Monica moves quickly to the table.*)

Monica: Yes, sir.

Maurice: Martha ...

Monica: "Monica," sir!

Maurice: Well, Monica. Take Mr. Bigelow's cocktail order, but first, button up your front!

(*Waitress looks down, quickly turns around and buttons her blouse. Maurice winks at Homer and walks off stage.*)

Monica: Sir?

Bigelow: Well, Monica. The Undersecretary Mr. Wheeler desires a "Wheeler Special," whatever that might be ...

Monica: Yes, sir. A double vodka martini, straight up, olive. (*In a low voice.*) The bartender knows him quite well!

Bigelow: Sounds fine ... Make it two ..

Monica: Yes, sir. Two doubles ...

Bigelow: And Monica, I'll have mine with a large olive—a very large olive.

Monica: Yes, sir! Two Wheeler Specials, one with a jumbo olive

(*Maurice appears in time to hear the order, and the waitress departs.*)

Maurice: (*Handing Bigelow a menu*) A Wheeler Special! Never fear, Homer. I'll see you back to your office ... Safe, but broke. (*Laughs, but then gets serious.*) Homer, old friend. Something's real strange here. I'm probably out of line, but (*lowers his voice*) Monica, well, she isn't one of ours. Boss brought her in late this morning and said "Morris, no questions!" My gut tells me your old friend Wheeler is getting set up ... if you know my meaning. Better take care ...

Bigelow: (*Smiling*) Thanks, Morry. Warning much appreciated, but nothing to worry about. Re-member me ... the cautious bureaucrat?

Maurice: (*Returning the smile*) OK, Homer. Sounds as if you know the game plan. Old Morry just hopes you don't get caught out of bounds. Hus-tling is a contact sport in Washington.

Bigelow: Come on, Morry. You know me. When you've been a straight-arrow bureaucrat for thir-ty years, you can't change. (*Smiles*) My wife says I'll stay the same ... even in retirement ... which, by the way, is here and now. That's why today's lunch is on Wheeler.

Maurice: Congratulations!

(*Wheeler approaches and Bigelow quickly studies his menu.*)

Bigelow: And what might you suggest, Maurice?

Maurice: Our chef, Alberto, is known worldwide for his superb Tournedos Rossini, Mr. Bigelow.

Bigelow: Beef?

Wheeler: Homer! That's filet!

Bigelow: Rossini?

Maurice: Yes, as the undersecretary appreciates, filet steak with artichokes and foie gras in a truly superb Madeira sauce. I'm certain you'll find it excellent.

Bigelow: Done. Sounds great.

Maurice: And the undersecretary?

Wheeler: Later, Maurice. And goose the waitress ... what's her name?

Maurice: Monica.

Wheeler: Well, goose Monica on our drinks.

Maurice: Yes, sir. Thank you, sir. (*Departs as the waitress arrives.*)

Monica: Sorry, sir ... had a bit of a problem finding a jumbo.

Wheeler: Jumbo?

Bigelow: For me. I like a jumbo olive ... soaks up the vodka.

Wheeler: (*Laughing*) That's old Homer .... Always cautious. Not today, old buddy. We're in a celebrating mode. Millie...

Monica: "Monica," sir.

Wheeler: Well, Monica, let's have a couple more of these in about ten minutes. Got it?

Monica: Yes, sir, Mr. Wheeler. And sir (*Addressing Bigelow*) ... I hope the olive is suitable.

Bigelow: Looks perfect. Thanks, Monica. And hold my order until Mr. Wheeler is ready.

Monica: Yes, sir. Thank you, gentlemen. (*Departs*)

Wheeler: That Baker! Jim's some guy! White House Chief of Staff, Homer. We've become great pals. Get in a set of tennis at least once a week. That is, if the president doesn't grab him to play cowboy at Ft. Meyer. Hey, Homer, don't ever quote your old buddy, for Christ's sake. (*Lowers his voice as Maurice approaches with a telephone.*)

Maurice: Mr. Undersecretary ...

Wheeler: (*Waving Maurice off*) Not yet, Maurice.

(*Continues his conversation with Bigelow as Maurice stands politely aside.*)

Wheeler: (*Speaking in a low voice*) Homer, consider this as strictly confidential. Just between a couple of old buddies. Jim just asked me if I could get our friends in congress to increase corporate entitlements by at least a third ... (*Smiles*) ... When I whispered in his ear, "You damn right I can, Jim," he whispered back, "You do that, Brad, before the end of this term, and you just might find a nice promotion in your future." (*He leans back in his chair with a smug look and then turns to Maurice.*) Well, Maurice ... ?

Maurice: Sorry, sir. The White House is trying ...

Wheeler: (*Jumping up and grabbing the telephone.*) Dammit, Maurice. Why didn't you say so ... We don't keep the president waiting. Hello? Yes, this is Wheeler ... Thank you ... Yes ... But ... I'm sorry ... Yes, I appreciate ... (*He holds the phone away from his ear. He hangs up and hands the telephone to Maurice, who has been standing by at a discrete distance.*) Take this damn thing, Maurice. Why didn't you tell me it wasn't the president! Oh! Forget it... (*He sits as Maurice speaks.*)

Maurice: My apologies, Mr. Undersecretary.

(*Maurice departs. There is a brief silence before Bigelow speaks.*)

Bigelow: Well, Brad. What the hell was that all about ... if you're free to say?

Wheeler: (*Scowling*) Mice! God ... damn ... mice!

Bigelow: (*Puzzled look*) Mice?

Wheeler: Mice! That's what I said ... Goddamn mice in the Lincoln Bedroom. (*Smiles*) That was our First Lady, Homer. So goddamn mad I couldn't get a word in ...

Bigelow: The First Lady! Why is she calling you?

Wheeler: She wasn't. Probably asked for Beeler, and they tracked-down Wheeler.

Bigelow: (*Laughing*) Tad Beeler ... Administrator of General Services. Did she finally understand she had Wheeler not Beeler?

Wheeler: Hell no! No chance before she slammed the damn phone down. (*Laughs*) Nearly busted my eardrum!

Bigelow: Hadn't you better call back and explain?

Wheeler: Hell no. I'll wander over and tell my buddy, Jim Baker. As chief of staff he commands the war on mice. He'll set things straight. Happened before. Right after the inaugural, I was summoned to the White House ... supposed to have brought carpet samples. When I explained to Ronnie and Nancy that I was the undersecretary of corporate entitlements and they needed to discuss the matter with Beeler, the head of general services, they apologized ... even invited me to stay for tea. (*Laughs*) Hell, Homer, when the First Lady finds she made an ass of herself, I may even get invited to a state dinner! Hang in there, Homer, while I see Baker ... And goose that amazon on the drinks. (*Leaves the table and, when out of sight, Maurice returns.*)

Maurice: (*With a wide grin*) There you have it, Homer. Never know what to expect at the Maison Rouge.

Bigelow: You're bad; you knew that wasn't the president calling ...

Maurice: (*Still grinning*) We never, never interrupt a pontificating politician ... of which our undersecretary is one of the best performing ...

Bigelow: (*Laughing*) How well I know!

Maurice: (*Getting serious*) Yeah ... The Maison Rouge gets all types. Every administration brings in the bad as well as the good ... Some of the country's best who come to do what they believe is good for the country. Others ... well, we do get the Wheelers ... those who place self-interest above all else ...

Bigelow: Am I hearing Morry the Philosopher letting it all hang out?

Maurice: (*Smiling*) It comes from once tending bar ... I've never forgotten Kennedy's inaugural speech. Morry's Chilli Parlor stayed open, but I stayed by the radio. Can't forget that line: "Ask not what your country can do for you; ask what you can do for your country."

Bigelow: I remember ... I stood in the cold ... froze my butt ... I've heard all the inaugural speeches since Eisenhower, and Kennedy's has to rank as the best.

Maurice: Guess Wheeler missed the event ... or the message ... Whoops ... Here comes your old buddy. (*Raises his voice.*) Yes, Mr. Bigelow. I'll see that Monica brings your drinks immediately. (*Bows to Wheeler and withdraws.*)

Wheeler: End of crises. Jim had a big laugh and said he'd fix things with the First Lady. Now where was I?

Bigelow: I got the idea you might be headed for a promotion. Secretary?

Wheeler: You got it, old buddy! The cabinet! Then Wall Street and mighty big ... MIGHTY BIG bucks.(*Leans back, smiles, and downs the remains of his martini.*)

Bigelow: Congratulations, Brad. I know you've worked ... will work hard for all you seek.

Wheeler: Well, thanks, Homer. Compliment accepted. (*Tips his empty glass as a toast.*) Nice to know at least one bureaucrat appreciates at least one politician. (*Laughs*) Now where's that damn waitress?

Bigelow: (*Looking across the room*) Headed this way.

(*Monica serves two martinis and starts to remove Bigelow's half-empty glass.*)

Bigelow: Monica, you can leave mine. I'm a slow drinker.

Monica: Yes, sir. (*Departs with Wheeler's empty glass.*)

Bigelow: (*Looking across the room.*) Interesting scenery ...

Wheeler: (*Turning to gaze in the same direction.*) You bet! Something to stir the juices ... Takes the mind off all the work waiting back at the office.

Bigelow: The blonde's not what I had in mind. It's this place ... the Maison Rouge. You've certainly moved out of my league since your BuSig days. Looks like Art Buchwald's with your friend Baker. Even better, (*Smiles*) isn't that Senator Scottsdale (*Nods towards the entrance*) with two young ladies?

Wheeler: Sure as hell is ... Old Scottsdale with a couple constituents. (*Laughs*) When he gets settled back in his office—if he manages—I've got to see him. He chairs my appropriations subcommittee, and if I'm to get more bucks for Corporate Entitlements, he's my man ... Try again, Homer. That's not Buchwald with Baker ... the guy's Pat Buchanan.

Bigelow: (*Squinting*) Sure is. Big time journalist and TV star ...

Wheeler: ... Only to pay the rent. Pat's first love is politics. Speechwriter for Nixon, stood by him all the way, right up to the end. Talk is that Pat's seeking support, for elective office. (*Smiles*) Yeah, even the White House. Don't smile, Homer. Could be. (*Leans over and lowers his voice.*) Homer, focus on the table to Baker's right, the redhead with the young stud ...

Bigelow: With the weird hat?

Wheeler: Right. Get this, Homer. Betcha the guy's a shill—hired for the occasion. She's not listening to him ... she's wired to eavesdrop on Baker and Buchanan. She happens to be the gossip columnist for the *Post*. In that nutty hat is a sound pickup!

Bigelow: You can't be serious?

Wheeler: No shit! Baker clued me in at tennis ... that's why I had to whisper in his ear ...

Bigelow: So why ...

Wheeler: Why talk? It's a game, old buddy. She needs crap for her column; they give her what they want. We all play the game, Homer. Fun with the lunch bunch. Hey, buddy, enough of this Washington crap! What's up at BuSig? Aren't you about to go out with a bang? Didn't I read that you're all for burning the Constitution? (*Laughs*)

Bigelow: (*Laughing*) Not quite! But we're still fighting a losing battle on the records front ... documents stacked to the ceiling. I goofed by suggesting to a house committee that some of these documents be destroyed. A half-baked ... or half-asleep ... reporter tied it to the Constitution and Declaration of Independence. You'd be amazed at the number of historians who sent letters protesting ...

Wheeler: So, get more storage space.

Bigelow: Not easy to do. Besides, we could never keep up with the volume, not as long as we're required by law to retain originals. We did get a rider last year ... only a seven-year hold on run-of-the-mill records. But some historians even protested that ... But what caused the uproar is when I suggested to the committee that many—not all, certainly not such historical documents as the Constitution and the Declaration of Independence—be copied, that the originals be destroyed rather than be lost to bugs, acid, and pickers.

Wheeler: Pickers?

Bigelow: Pickers! Those good people who come to BuSig to do research. Some frauds, most not, but slip out with a few signed documents. Some to keep, some to sell. When a Gerald Ford signature brings two, three hundred on the autograph market, you get an idea of what we're up against.

Wheeler: And you call them "pickers."

Bigelow: Pickers are a special breed. Collectors have been known to place their order with a picker. It's like the underground car market. You covet a Mercedes SL? ... Place your order with an auto "picker," and he'll go out and steal precisely what your little old thieving heart desires. Require a Harry Truman to round out your presidential collection? Place your order with a picker and he'll pay a visit to BuSig ...

Wheeler: (*Gulping his martini.*) So ... you'd destroy the originals?

Bigelow: Not all ... most. Those not of any great historical significance. The Constitution, treaties, Emancipation Proclamation, and the like ... these we save and keep well protected. Why spend millions—someday billions—protecting original documents that few people ever see once filed? Hell, even with the Constitution, most viewers are more impressed with the fancy display case than with the words. One might argue that the money could be better spent on education than a show of old paper memorabilia ...

Wheeler: Yeah ... guess you're right. Who the hell would bother to steal a copy?

Bigelow: You got it! By the way, Brad, you've never told me how you got on the Nixon-Agnew bandwagon and landed at BuSig.

Wheeler: Short version: Came out of Penn, landed with a stockbroker in Philly. Pretty good money with no heavy lifting but dull as hell. Had lunch one day with an old prep school buddy up from Baltimore. Heard my sad tale and asked if I'd like to do advance work for the vice president in the coming '72 campaign. (*Laughs*) I asked, "What the hell is 'advance work?'" ... Whatever the candidate wants! Lousy pay, great payoff ... If he wins! Like betting on one roll of the dice. You lose, nothing; you win ... Well, like my old buddy said, "Opportunities unlimited!"

Bigelow: (*Smiling*) Like landing a plush job at BuSig?

Wheeler: Crap! Deserved a hellava lot better. Ted said he'd take care of me ... something big ...

Bigelow: But his resignation interfered. Right?

Wheeler: You know it! I'll let you in on something, Homer. Ted Agnew would have made one fine president. Sure as hell better than Gerry Ford.

Bigelow: Come again? What I recall ... besides his legal trouble ... were his battles with the press. That "nattering nabob" and "pusillanimous pussyfooters."

Wheeler: Politics! Pure politics. That came from the Nixon-Agnew speechwriters during the '72 campaign. Our old friend over there, Pat Buchanan, provided the "pussyfooter" line and Bill Safire, now with the *New York Times*, the "nattering nabobs of negativism"—a pretty good description, I might add, of the liberal press that hounded us. But Ted could have written his own speeches had he the time. He's damn sharp. Ford couldn't carry his bags.

Bigelow: His own speechwriter? (*Smiles*) No doubt like George Wallace with his "pointy-headed bureaucrats" and "pseudo-intellectuals."

Wheeler: (*Obviously irritated*) Come off that crap, Homer. Show some respect where it's due. Ted played a positive role during the first term and in getting Nixon re-elected. The guy's got a first-rate mind. You bet, Ford sure as hell couldn't carry his bags ...

Bigelow: Speaking of bags ... didn't I read recently that Agnew got socked by a judge to anti-up a cool quarter million as payback to Maryland for bribes and kickbacks?

Wheeler: Pure crap! That was nothing but partisan politics! Ted played by the established Maryland rules. You damnbureaucrats are blind to the real world and ignore all he really accomplished.

Bigelow: Such as ...? Hand me a "for instance."

Wheeler: OK! Take the space program, old buddy. Ted was the chairman of the president's Space Task Group. Really poured his heart into it ... way ahead of the doubters. Solidly behind the proposed missions to Mars ... Something von Braun really appreciated.

Bigelow: OK, chalk up one ...

Wheeler: And the astronauts ... they sure appreciated Ted. Gene Ceman was a golfing partner. Ted even dined with the family at their home in Houston during the campaign. Still keeps in touch ...

Bigelow: Interesting! Hadn't heard …

Wheeler: (*Showing emotion*) Yessir, Homer. You better believe Spiro Agnew would have made a damn fine president. And he sure as hell would have beat Jimmy Carter in '76.

Bigelow: (*Smiling*) And handed Bradley Wheeler a bigger job in '77?

Wheeler: You damn well know it! Hey, old buddy, no more arguing. I'm happy. I'm in with a real winner in Ronald Reagan. Could be the best since Eisenhower. Look at the talent he's brought in: General Al Haig at State, Ray Donovan over at Labor, Sam Pierce—sure as hell, one of the country's top Blacks—at HUD. And don't forget Jim Watt at Interior. These are the kind of guys that can clean up the mess left by Jimmy Carter and his Georgia crackers. (*Smiles*) That is, if the damnbureaucrats don't screw up the effort!

Bigelow: Good thing we "damnbureaucrats" come thick-skinned. If things do get better, you politicians take full credit … And if things go bad, here we are …

Wheeler: Now, don't get upset, old buddy. I know you; you're an exception. Now tell me … how'd a talented guy like you ever become a damnbureaucrat?

Bigelow: (*Smiling*) Call it pure good fortune! Came out of the army ... Landed a degree in history courtesy of the GI Bill. A professor suggested I try BuSig as a good alternative to putting students to sleep teaching history in high school. Took the civil service exam ... lonely place in the examining room. Government salaries low in the fifties ... Most of my classmates headed for industry and big bucks—at least that's what they expected. Anyhow, I landed with BuSig as an archivist trainee and, as the saying goes, floated up the ladder. Never regretted the decision ... loved the work. May even teach history somewhere down the road. Hey, Brad! How about we eat? (*Waitress approaches with a tray of martinis.*) Oh, oh! I see trouble coming!

Monica: Mr. Wheeler, compliments of Ms. McFee.

Wheeler: Rosebud! Good old Rosie! She's my favorite. Rosie runs the Washington office of the Smokeless Tobacco Association. Best damn party-giver in town. (*Rises unsteadily.*) I got to go pay my respects to my old buddy, Rosebud ... Excuse ...

Bigelow: Food, Brad. Food ...

Wheeler: (*Speech slurred.*) Go ahead, Homer. Hey Mabel ... Monica. (*Monica returns.*) Oh, forget it. I'll be right back.

(After Wheeler and Monica depart, Bigelow eats his jumbo olive, pours his martini into his water glass, then adds an olive from his pocket that contains a miniature microphone, and tests it.)

Bigelow: *(Whispering)* Testing, 1-2-3.

(Maurice returns to the table.)

Maurice: *(Smiling)* Homer, you're a fraud.

Bigelow: *(Mocked surprise)* Me? ... A fraud?

Maurice: Maurice sees all ... part of the job. You ain't had a sip since you came in, and your buddy's practically walking on the ceiling. I'll bet your water glass is loaded.

Bigelow: Now, Morry, surely you won't tell. *(Pauses to stare at a man who shuffles by, head down.)* Good lord! What is that?

Maurice: *(Laughing)* That, my fraudulent friend, is none other than G. Dudley Liverpool. Yale '36 ... Top spy, so they say, in WWII. Late, so they also say, of the CIA.

Bigelow: Ah! Central Intelligence Agency.

Maurice: That's the outfit. One of America's leading spooks. Has all the right connections ... Fancy New England prep school ... Old Boy's Club ... First name bases with all the old gentlemen spooks: Dulles, Colby ... Once lunched regularly with Dr. Schlesinger when he was in town.

Bigelow: Schlesinger? The Harvard historian? Worked in the Kennedy White House? What's his connection with the CIA?

Maurice: The Old Boy's Club. Ex-spooks from the Second World War ... the OSS ..

Bigelow: OSS ... Office of Strategic Services ...

Maurice: You got it! They're organized ... meet regularly ... sometimes at the Maison Rouge. Probably tell war stories ... Hot and cold war stories, I'll bet ...

Bigelow: I gather from his appearance, old G. Dudley Liverpool has been dropped from the club. What happened?

Maurice: (*Smiling*) The way old Morris heard it, poor old Dudley liked a bit of strange ... Seems he dropped in over on Thomas Circle ... had his jollies ... fell asleep and missed a very important lunch appointment.

Bigelow: At the Maison Rouge, no doubt.

Maurice: At the Maison Rouge. Story is unconfirmed, but makes sense. Old Dudley was to meet the highest ranking Commie defector yet— waaay up in the Kremlin, like a son to Breshnev, all that crap. Yeah, poor old Dudley blew it. The Russian, nervous as hell, waited at least an hour ... some say, two ... (*Grins*) The story keeps

getting better! The latest version has Ivan down-
ing ten shots straight vodka. Took off. (*Laughs*)
... probably flying. No one has seen him since ...
over a year.

Bigelow: And old Dudley won't give up, right?

Maurice: Right! Dudley comes back first Tuesday
of every month. Twelve noon, waits one hour.
Three stingers, visits the men's room, leaves.
Each month he looks a bit worse. Yeah, Homer.
A lot of interesting goings on here at the Maison
Rouge. Wanna write a book?

Bigelow: Nope! Got my own weird tales to tell.
CIA sack him?

Maurice: Doubt it. Strange outfit ... And here
comes old Dudley back from his piss ...

(*As Dudley reaches the table, he suddenly stops, snatch-
es Homer's jumbo olive, gulps it down, and marches
off stage. Maurice struggles to keep from bursting out
laughing.*)

Bigelow: My ... mmm ... my jumbo ... He ate my
jumbo olive!

Maurice: (*Still laughing*) Homer, you just stood
Dudley Liverpool to lunch. Never fear. I'll send
over a replacement on the house ... surrounded
by vodka! (*Departs laughing as Monica moves hur-
riedly to the table.*)

Monica: (*In a loud whisper*) What happened? You were coming through loud and clear ... suddenly we got the strangest sounds ...

Bigelow: You were picking up Liverpool ...

Monica: What? Liverpool! We can't ...

Bigelow: Forget it. Any backup for the olive? Wheeler's ripe for the sting ...

Monica: Try this! (*Hands Bigelow a fountain pen.*) Just don't let him use it to sign the check.

Bigelow: I'll remember.

(*Monica departs as Wheeler returns.*)

Wheeler: That Rosebud is something, old buddy. If I wasn't a happily married family man ... Hey! This martini is calling my name. (*Downs half the drink.*) Homer, old buddy, how'd things go at BuSig when the Carter people took over? You make out OK?

Bigelow: Sure, Brad. You know me. I always get along with my political bosses ...

Wheeler: (*Slurred speech*) Bosses, hell! You guys ... you damnbureaucrats ... (*Laughs*) That's one word ... like damnyankees ... You guys really work for yourselves ... (*Laughs louder*) Self ... employed on the government's payroll ...

Bigelow: (*Obviously irritated*) Come on, Brad. You know better ...

Wheeler: Hell I do! You damnbureaucrats have mastered the art of not taking orders ...

Bigelow: (*Obviously annoyed*) Look, Brad. I've been around the government some thirty odd years. I understand what bugs you and most politicians coming from outside the beltway. You come in to take over—Eisenhower, Kennedy, less so Johnson, certainly Nixon and Carter. They come in with a mandate ... millions of votes ... to get things done. Make changes. Reorganize the executive branch. Cut red tape. Kick bureaucratic ass. It follows as night follows day ...

Wheeler: And they run up against a bureaucratic wall; damnbureaucrats telling the president and his people what they can't do.

Bigelow: If you're into damning, try damning the US Constitution. That cherished document has more ways of stymieing the president than we damnbureaucrats can ever cook up ... Even Ike—a well-trained military bureaucrat—discovered he had more real authority as a general than handed him as president. (*Smiles as Monica approaches.*) Hey, old buddy. Let's declare a truce and enjoy our lunch! OK?

(*Wheeler sulks.*)

Monica: Gentlemen ... May I take your order?

Bigelow: Monica, I'll have Maison Rouge's famous Tournedos Rossini.

Monica: Excellent choice, sir. With asparagus?

Bigelow: Sounds fine ...

Monica: Appetizer? Salad, perhaps?

Bigelow: No appetizer. Salad with your house dressing.

Monica: Very good, sir. Mr. Wheeler?

Wheeler: (*Sullen*) No appetizer. Poached salmon. Small potatoes. Asparagus.

Monica: Yes, sir. Thank you, sir.

Wheeler: And a bottle of the Chablis I had last week.

Monica: Very good, sir.

Wheeler: ... and coffee ... hazelnut ... and brandy, later.

Monica: Certainly, sir. (*Departs*)

Bigelow: (*Raises his glass*) Still friends, Brad?

Wheeler: Hell yes, old buddy. (*Pauses*) I guess what still bugs me is how you ... bureaucrats ... stuck it to Nixon ...

Bigelow: Come again, Brad. Impeachment ...

Wheeler: No, no! Not that! I'm talking about BuSig ... Nixon donating his vice president's papers ... How you screwed him out of a tax deduction.

Bigelow: Hold on! Tilt! You seem to have forgotten the facts. Congress, not BuSig, slammed the door on those fat deductions. Deductions, I might add, that never made sense ...

Wheeler: Made sense for LBJ ... That, you damn well know, advised Nixon to do the same!

Bigelow: Perhaps, perhaps not. Anyway, what I'm saying is that the idea of government documents, produced by government officials while doing the government's business ... Dammit, Brad, these ought not be considered private property to keep ... to destroy ... sure as hell, not to donate and take a big, fat tax deduction. And that is exactly why a law was passed in 1969 and stopped the practice!

Wheeler: But you damn well know that Nixon donated his papers before 1969, before your anti-Nixon law was passed.

Bigelow: Only to store, old buddy! Nixon's people ... 1961. .. '62 ... simply stuffed folders in boxes and dumped 'em on BuSig. We had no instructions, no idea as to what he had in mind. Maybe donate them to a college ... save 'em for his heirs ... burn 'em. We had no instructions, simply waiting to be told what to do ... where to ship 'em ...

Wheeler: Crap! Crap! More bureaucratic crap! You had the goddamn papers. Some idiot on Nixon's staff just screwed-up ... should have signed 'em over, as I tried to tell you ...

(*Monica approaches and presents the wine to Wheeler.*)

Monica: Mr. Wheeler, Les Clos '61?

Wheeler: Looks OK.

(*Monica fills glasses and departs.*)

Bigelow: (*Sips his wine.*) Very good! Thanks, Brad. Look. I appreciate this is a sore point ... I remember how it bugged you at the time. But Richard Nixon's vice presidential papers became the property of BuSig ... the US government ... when legally conveyed. And that is exactly why this damnbureaucrat refused to accept a backdated document ...

Wheeler: Bullshit! Nitpicking! What the hell's the difference? You had the goddamn papers. Richard Nixon sure as hell deserved no less than Lyndon Johnson. That SOB got one hellava tax break!

Bigelow: As the law then allowed. But the law was changed, and Nixon's papers were conveyed after the cutoff. Sorry, but we bureaucrats don't make the law ...

Wheeler: Like hell you don't! You guys pick and choose all the time. Apply what you like and ignore the rest. (*Laughs*) Isn't that the way your old bureaucratic buddy J. Edgar Hoover ran the FBI for years? And there wasn't anything any president ... even Nixon ... could do about it!

Bigelow: (*Smiling*) Touché! Hoover's in a class all alone. Sure ... there are bureaucrats ... none that I know ... that may set themselves above the law. But that really is the exception. If it were left to me ... or to any BuSig archivist, all official documents would stay with the government. (*Laughs*) And that would require another large building to house all that Henry Kissinger carted away!

Wheeler: (*Speech even more slurred*) Aw, let's let it rest, old buddy. Ancient history ... dead horse. We're here to celebrate old Homer's release from government bondage. (*Raises his glass and grins.*) And maybe do his old buddy a favor. To Homer! To a long and happy retirement ... Cheers!

Bigelow: (*Raising his glass*) Cheers! Thanks, Brad. And may you find happiness in Corporate Entitlements ... or, at least, the path to all you desire. Now, what's this favor?

Wheeler: Later! Right now old Brad has to piss. (*Rises unsteadily as Monica arrives, serves their food, and refills the wine glasses.*) Go ahead, old buddy, and eat. I'll catch up.

Bigelow: Thanks, Brad. Food, I need.

(*Wheeler staggers off.*)

Monica: (*Speaking softly*) Loud and clear. All on tape.

Bigelow: Good! (*Laughs*) When old Dudley pinched my olive, our best laid plans ... Hey! Wheeler wants something from me ... Be alert 'cause I suspect he's ripe for the sting. (*Smiles*) Unless he passes out in the john! I'm going to bait him about the Agnew letter when he returns. If it works, and he tells us what we want ... come fast! He just might take a swing at me ...

Monica: I'll be here, never fear!

(*Male and female laughter erupts from a table behind the partition. Both men pause and the laughter dies.*)

Bigelow: Sounds like a pretty good party.

Monica: (*Leaning close and lowering her voice*) A pair of White House types. A light marine colonel and a woman who works for him. For God's sake don't quote me, but we've got them under surveillance ... Something to do with Iran and weapons to the Nicaraguan contras. Talk around the bureau is that it could be a bigger scandal than Watergate ...

Bigelow: That, the country can do without!

Monica: (*Smiling*) Well, it keeps some of us employed ...

(*Monica departs. Bigelow is eating as Wheeler staggers to the table.*)

Wheeler: Ran into that old goat, Scottsdale. (*Points to the entrance.*) There he goes with his two bimbos ... probably has a hard-on.

Bigelow: Bimbos? I thought you said they were a couple of the senator's constituents?

Wheeler: (*Laughing*) That's old straight-arrow Homer! Constituents! Every Tuesday he gets a pair over on Fourteenth Street ... Must come from a Rent-A-Constituent agency! (*Laughs harder*) I hear it's done in the back of his limo ... you guess how. (*Suddenly stops laughing and leans closer to Bigelow.*) Homer ... got to talk serious business, OK?

Bigelow: (*Stops eating and leans closer.*) Sure, Brad.

Wheeler: You know, we were talking about the Agnew letter, the missing resignation letter. Homer, what do you think its worth? You can tell your old buddy Brad ...

Bigelow: Sure, Brad. I'd guess five, maybe ten thousand in a few more years. If its truly authentic.

Wheeler: What'd you mean, authentic? 'Course its authentic ... nobody'd steal a copy ... you said that! You better believe it's the real thing!

Bigelow: Sure, probably is. All I'm saying is that someone might have been fooled by a copy ... I'd have to see it to be certain its authentic.

Wheeler: (*Leaning back in his chair with a wide grin.*) Well now, old buddy ... just maybe old Brad Wheeler ... just maybe your old buddy can do just that .. I just may know where that little old letter—now, I haven't got it—but I just may know where it might be had!

Bigelow: I need only one guess ...

Wheeler: (*Smirking*) Try!

Bigelow: Easy ... Spiro T. Agnew!

Wheeler: (*Frowning*) Agnew? Why'd you pick Ted? It's his letter ...

Bigelow: Hunch, mostly. Easy for Agnew to keep the original and send on a copy.

Wheeler: (*Heavy frown as he eats.*) Yeah, guess so ... But if Ted wanted the original, why'nt he just sign a second letter and keep the original? ... Or maybe sign four or five?

Bigelow: Value! ... Would drop the market value. More than one signed copy on the market and I withdraw what I said the letter was probably worth.

Wheeler: (*Breaking out in a big smile*) Gotcha! Boy, my old buddy sure knows his business. And old Ted Agnew would've been smart enough to figure that out!

Bigelow: And dealing with enough problems without adding morel But you bring up an interesting point ... Duplicate letters. A little advice, Brad. Don't buy a Nixon letter of resignation, if offered.

Wheeler: Fakes! Nixon fakes floating around?

Bigelow: Not fakes, duplicates. Its been established that Richard Nixon signed more than one letter resigning the presidency. How many? Who knows?

Wheeler: You putting me on, old buddy?

Bigelow: Not at all. Between you and me, Brad—strictly confidential—BuSig has, under lock and key, the Nixon original. As required by law it came to us through the State Department, duly initialed with an HK, Henry Kissinger. Then, about six months ago, someone noticed in an autograph dealer's catalog, Nixon's resignation letter up for sale ...

Wheeler: The real thing?

Bigelow: Real signature, no copy, no autopen. Spacing in the letter slightly different. It was offered by the dealer not as the letter of resignation but as a letter signed by Nixon. Since we have no idea as to how many such letters Nixon signed, the true value is anyone's guess. (*Laughing*) My advice, old buddy ... don't buy!

Wheeler: I'm with you, Homer. Now, here's something really confidential. How'd my old buddy like to see the Agnew letter, the real Spiro Agnew letter? (*Sits back with a smug look.*)

Bigelow: You serious?

Wheeler: Real serious, old buddy. Real serious!

Bigelow: I gather, Brad, you've got Spiro Agnew's letter of resignation from the office of vice president of the United States. Right?

Wheeler: I didn't say that! I said I could ... might ... show you the letter ... Get you to tell me if it really is authentic ... That's what I said.

Bigelow: (*Standing and speaking in a loud voice*) Well, old buddy. That's enough. If you can show me the letter, you can give me what belongs ... not to you ... not to who you may represent. That letter, Mr. Wheeler, as set forth in law, belongs in the

Bureau of Significant Documents ... held there
on behalf of the people ... present and future ... of
these United States!

Wheeler: (*Appears stunned, then jumps up, upsetting
his chair.*) Homer! You ... You ... damnbureaucrat.
I could ...

(*Wheeler is grabbed by Monica.*)

Monica: FBI! You are under arrest. You have a right
to remain silent. You have a right to an attorney.
What you say may be used in evidence against
you.

Wheeler: (*Still struggling*) Old buddy ... You're a
real shit!

(*Wheeler is escorted out by FBI agent Monica as Maurice, who has been watching, comes to Bigelow.*)

Maurice: Homer, it looks like you just cost us one
of our best customers!

Bigelow: Sir! (*Bows*) May I offer my deepest
apologies?

Maurice: (*Laughing*) I'm certain the Maison Rouge
will survive the loss. Bury one Wheeler in
Washington and a dozen rise outta the muck!

Bigelow: (*Sighing*) I'm afraid you're right, Morry. Let's get together ... down the avenue ... I'll buy you a beer and fill you in on the sad, sad saga of *BuSig v. Bradley Foster Wheeler the Third.* Meanwhile (*Extends his hand*) I'd better be off ...

Maurice: (*Shakes hands but has one hand behind his back.*) We'll do that, Homer. But meanwhile, Maurice who sees all, knows all has a little something for you from the Maison Rouge ...

Bigelow: (*Puzzled expression*) Oh?

Maurice: (*Bowing*) Sir, your check!

(*Bigelow looks at the check, frowns, and then looks up at Maurice and smiles. Maurice returns the smile, and they head offstage arm in arm as Bigelow speaks.*)

Bigelow: Looks as if you'll have to buy the beer, Morry!

(*Stage darkens.*)

PLAYREADERS PRESENTS:

The Resurrection of Louise Brooks

1906 - 1985

One of the most mysterious and potent figures in the cinema… She was one of the first performers to penetrate the heart of screen acting.

A FILM CRITIC

Script by
ROBERT HUDDLESTON
Adapted from *Louise Brooks* by Barry Paris

Thursday, April 17
7:30 pm
CM Auditorium

The Resurrection of Louise Brooks

1906–1985

*One of the most mysterious and potent figures
in the cinema … She was one of the first performers
to penetrate the heart of screen acting.*
– A FILM CRITIC

Adapted from Louise Brooks *by Barry Paris, 1989*

Louise Brooks...

... as actress: Those who have seen her can never forget her. She is the modern actress par excellence ... As soon as she takes the screen, fiction disappears along with art, and one has the impression of being present at a documentary. The camera seems to have caught her by surprise, without her knowledge. She is the intelligence of the cinematic process, the perfect incarnation of that which is photogenic; she embodies all that the cinema rediscovered in the last years of silence: complete naturalness and complete simplicity. Her art is so pure that it becomes invisible.

> – *Henri Langlois, director of the Cinémathêque Française*

... as a writer: [*writing about W.C. Fields*] He was an isolated person. As a young man, he stretched out his hand to Beauty and Love and they thrust it away. Gradually he reduced reality to exclude all but his work, filling the gaps with alcohol, whose dim eyes transformed the world into a distant view of harmless shadows. He was also a solitary person. Years of traveling alone around the world with his juggling act taught him the value of solitude and the release it gave his mind ... Most of his life will remain unknown. But the history of no life is a jest.

The Play

Scene One: Set in Louise's apartment in New York in the early 1950s

Scene Two: Set in her apartment in Rochester, NY, in the late 1950s

The Set

There are two scenes, but both use the same set: two chairs with a small table. The chair and table, right of center stage, is in Louise Brooks's apartment in New York. The table holds a gin bottle and glass and several books. The chair at center stage left is occupied by James Card. He first speaks to the audience then moves to be close to Louise. The second scene takes place in an apartment in Rochester, New York. A small table has been added with a typewriter, several files, and a telephone. The first scene is set in the early 1950s, the second in the late 1950s. To note the change between scenes, the stage lights will dim then rise.

The Cast

Louise Brooks: a once beautiful silent screen actress now in her early fifties as the play opens, looking much older.

James Card: film curator at the George Eastman Museum of Film in Rochester, New York. He is in his mid-forties. His interest in Louise Brooks began with the preservation of her films for the Eastman film archives then moves forward to aiding her in publishing her experiences in Hollywood and abroad. His ultimate goal is to induce her to publish an autobiography.

"General" Oscar Solbert: director of Eastman House. Has a brief appearance. "General" is an honorific, based only on the fact that he had served in both World Wars I and II.

The Play

Scene One

The play opens with a film of Louise Brooks's performance in the German silent movie *Pandora's Box.* Louise is in her chair drinking gin and reading.

James Card enters the stage, sits in the chair at stage left and speaks as the film fades from the screen.

Card: I'm James Card, curator of film at the George Eastman Museum at Rochester, New York. I am deeply involved in locating and preserving film, especially early motion pictures. That quest took me to Paris in 1955 to meet with Henri Langlois from the Cinematheque, a gentleman with identical interests. I recall vividly his reaction when I explained I was seeking early films featuring Greta Garbo and Marlene Dietrich. He responded as only a Frenchman can, with arms waving.

"There is no Garbo! There is no Dietrich!" he declared. "There is only Louise Brooks!"

Louise Brooks? It took a while but soon I recalled a movie—it was in the 1930s—I can't remember either the name or plot, but I still have a vision of the beautiful heroine with coal-black hair with bangs.

Courtesy of Messrs. Langlois, I soon had a special viewing of Louise Brooks in *Pandora's Box* and *Diary of a Lost Girl*, both filmed in Berlin, the first in 1928, the second in 1929, by the great German director G.W. Pabst. From that moment on, I knew I had to locate and interview this amazing actress. A friend in the theater in

New York produced her address but doubted she would see me. He described her as living in a depressing one-room apartment on West Fifty-First Street. A chronic drinker, her bitterness had destroyed her beauty and lovely body. Despite that, I explained I was a film historian and described my visit to Paris where they had restored her stardom ... And that I wanted to visit her and learn the story of her acting career, especially her films in Berlin. After a few days, I received her response.

Louise: "Dear Mr. Card, Thank you for your letter. You, after almost thirty years, bring me the first joy I ever tasted from my movie career. You see, they didn't know what to do with me when I arrived in Hollywood in 1925. After a screen test, they laughed and kidded me about my acting. I vowed I would never see a picture I was in— and I never have, not even my pictures made in Europe.

Card: (*Speaking to the audience*) We exchanged numerous letters, advancing from "Dear Mr. Card" to "Dear Jimmy" when she finally agreed to my coming for a visit, which I did on October 23, 1955. What did I expect? I was told she lived in a gloomy one-room apartment. Well it was one room, but it was meticulously clean and scrubbed. With a strong smell of gin. She received me barefooted, dressed in a nightgown ...

and admitted she spent most of her time in bed reading. That said, we took an immediate and powerful liking to each other.

Louise: Well, Mr. Jimmy Card, now I know what you look like.

Card: Satisfied?

Louise: (Smiling) Very satisfied. But I don't know why I need you, or anyone else, to assist me in writing a book about Hollywood. As I wrote to you, I do know how to write.

Card: And what have you written?

Louise: (With a laugh) My autobiography.

Card: Published?

Louise: No.

Card: Might I read the manuscript?

Louise: No ... l threw it into an incinerator. I shall never write my memoirs!

Card: And why is that, Louise?

Louise: Not now, Jimmy. Perhaps someday ... but not now.

Card: If you prefer. Now ... why I have been so anxious to meet you. I want to know what was behind your landing the role of Lulu and your experience in acting under the direction of the director G.W. Pabst. Only then can I fully understand the movie *Pandora's Box*, a classic of the silent screen. And, as if this isn't enough, I'd like to learn of your experiences in Hollywood— the persons you met and respected and those at the other end ...

Louise: (*Pours a half glass of gin and takes a sip.*) 1925. I was nineteen. I had moved from my home in Kansas to New York at fifteen as a dancer with the great dance team, Denishawn. I learned to act by watching the wonderful Martha Graham dance, and I learned to dance by watching Charlie Chaplin act.

Card: And how long were you with Denishawn?

Louise: After two years I found the discipline stifling, and they couldn't tolerate my behavior. So, I was sacked!. My dancing got me into the chorus line in George White's Scandals and the Follies. That lasted for two years, and it was the most enjoyable period of my young life.

Card: How so?

Louise: The dancing, spectacular shows. The girls I worked with were great. We weren't paid much but lived and dressed well, courtesy of wealthy stage-door Johnnies. (*Laughing*) And Jimmy, I had some great love affairs. (*Still laughing*) When a girl had a one-night affair, we talked about doing the "horizontal Charleston." Some of the Johnnies headed to Florida to escape the cold New York weather and took several of the chorus along.

Card: That sounds appealing.

Louise: More than that ... a couple of millionaires provided Ziegfeld with money to produce Palm Beach Nights, a small edition of the Follies. We began in the town of Ocala. Nobody in Ocala seemed to have heard of Prohibition, and the gin flowed like water. A few "shoots" in Ocala and we were off to Palm Beach, where we staged our mini-Follies in a night club. One of the chorus was Paulette Goddard, who later married Charlie Chaplin, and Susan Fleming, who married Harpo Marx.

Card: And then ...

Louise: That led to Hollywood. What a change! My New York friends were literary people—I was even introduced to Scott and Zelda Fitzgerald. But in Hollywood there seemed to be no one who read books. I went to the bookstore on Hollywood Boulevard, and these Hollywood people would go in and say, "I have a bookshelf, and I want to buy enough books to fill the shelves." And that is the reading they did. So for me, Hollywood came to be terrible roles, great parties, interesting people ... Charlie Chaplin—a great actor, a wonderful friend, and beautiful lover. W.C. Fields. Wallace Beery. Buster Keaton. Even

the disgraced Roscoe Arbuckle, who was a great
director and a magnificent actor.

Card: Fatty Arbuckle ... wasn't he convicted of rape
and murder?

Louise: No! He was tried for manslaughter but
never convicted. In fact, following his acquittal
the jury wrote him a letter apologizing for his
having been charged. But Hollywood rarely dealt
in facts, usually in impressions, many fed by
studio propaganda. The result is that the public
absorbs the impression: sexy on-screen, sexy
off-screen; virginal on-screen, virginal off-screen.
As for Arbuckle, I made one forgettable picture
with him, but in other films he was wonderful.
The public's mistaken impression destroyed him
in mind and body.

Card: I'm impressed with your knowledge and
insights.

Louise: Observe, listen, and remember. I made
many visits to Hearst's castle at San Simeon ...
you know, the newspaper mogul whose mistress
was Marian Davies. I met many people I liked
and respected, some I sought to avoid, including
Hearst. Met a talented director—Eddie Sutherland—and we married. Terrible mistake. But we
did give wonderful parties. At one—it was my
idea—all place cards at dinner were books. In
front of Irving Thalberg's place, I put Dreiser's

Genius. That's just before he married Norma Shearer. So in front of Norma's place I placed *The Difficulty of Getting Married.* It was so funny because Irving walked right in and saw *Genius* and sat down. But Norma kept walking around. She wouldn't sit down in front of *The Difficulty of Getting Married.* God, that was a fun evening.

Card: What an unusual dinner party ...

Louise: But not enough to salvage the marriage. I had married Eddie because he was a charming man who had besieged me with a gold band. He belonged heart and soul to Hollywood. Me, I was an alien. He loved parties—that kept us together as long as it lasted—but often he was off somewhere. And when we weren't giving or attending a party, he was a big bore ... so I went off to Florida for a vacation and met George Marshall. The Sutherland marriage was doomed.

Card: Marshall, the director ...

Louise: No! No! Not that Marshall. And not the General George Marshall. .. My George was George Preston Marshall. He's now the owner of the Washington Redskins football team. Back then he was a handsome, very wealthy young man, so we headed to Havana for a wonder- ful week ... the beginning of a long and lovely relationship. George understood my passion for books, and I fell in love with his mind. You could never get bored with George. That Havana week hastened my divorce from Eddie Sutherland

Card: (*Smiling*) Am I about to learn about Berlin?

Louise: Be patient, Jimmy, there is a connection. 1928. Budd Schulberg at Paramount had me under contract. Talkies were coming in, and it was his game to summon young actors and declare, "We don't know if your voice will cut it." So he'd cut your pay and say, "Take it or leave," thrusting the new contract at you. Well, unlike many others, I flat-out quit, and he was totally astonished ... but I stood firm. That was when he told me Pabst wanted me in Berlin to star in a new movie. George Marshall encouraged me to take the offer, so I got Schulberg to cable Pabst that I was available ...

Card: Appears that this George was pretty influential.

Louise: (*Smiling*) All my lovers, to a greater or lesser degree, had influence. His advice was: you're unhappy in Hollywood; go to Berlin and see what it offers. George had business in Europe and said he would escort me to Berlin.

Card: A nice arrangement.

Louise: You bet. Only George and Pabst never got along.

Card: And why was that?

Louise: *Pandora's Box*, being a silent film, had no script. And we had no rehearsals—no idea as to what each day's shoot would be. We'd show up; he would describe the scene and leave it to each character to respond. As Lulu, I got into it, and he liked what I did. What he didn't like was that George and I would do the town in the evening ... and what a town Berlin was! Sex was its main business. It made New York, even Hollywood, seem dull. Finally Mr. Pabst ordered me to stay in the night before the next shoot. I argued otherwise but finally gave in, so George decided to leave Berlin ...

Card: Pabst's style of directing would indicate that he had much confidence in his cast ... especially in the character Lulu.

Louise: Yes, and he later told me that he was about to cast Marlene Dietrich as Lulu, which would not have worked. She made one decent film, and that was *Blue Angel*. Her other films featured Marlene as Marlene.

Card: You're a tough critic.

Louise: As you will learn from my Hollywood story ...

Card: Louise, where did you learn to write? You said you were a sales clerk after you returned to New York in the 1940s. Did you attend classes in writing?

Louise: Jimmy, I knew even before I left home at fifteen that writing is a skill that evolves from reading. And reading in the Brooks house was a way of life. Our house was literally falling down with books. The foundation on the right side of the room where Father had his law books had sunk eleven inches from the weight of the books. There were books in the bedrooms, old books in the basement, and unread books in the living room. And in the library were the books I loved: Dickens, Thackeray, Tennyson, Carlyle, John Stuart Mill. And American authors: Emerson, Hawthorne, and Mark Twain. I inherited many wonderful books from that library.

Card: Well said! Now, Louise. Will you accept my advice and move to Rochester, where you can get started writing your Hollywood experiences?

Louise: Yes, Mr. Jimmy Card. I've decided Roch-ester might be an improvement over Fifty-First Street, although I'll miss my nightly gin and friends at Glennon's Bar.

Scene Two

The lights dim to indicate a change from Louise's apartment in New York to one in Rochester. Louise replaces the gin with a typewriter and files. Card moves to the back of stage, where Oscar Solbert has entered. As the lights are raised, Card leads Solbert to meet Louise.

Card: Louise, I'm pleased to introduce my boss, Oscar Solbert, director of George Eastman House. He has been most anxious to meet you ...

Louise: (*Shakes Solbert's hand.*) Can't understand why ... but thank you Mr. Solbert.

Solbert: Miss Brooks. I've truly been looking forward to this. A number of people have commented on your remarkable beauty and unusual acting career, especially in Europe.

Louise: Oh! And might I know my fans?

Solbert: (*Smiling*) Well, Miss Brooks ... may I call you Louise?

Louise: Please do, Oscar.

Solbert: Mr. William Paley—he's the head of the Columbia Broadcasting System ...

Louise: I'm well-aware of Bill Paley. He happens to be a long-time friend and benefactor. And, I'm pleased to say, an unforgettable lover ...

Solbert: (*Not quite certain as to how to respond.*) Yes, of course … Mr. Paley urged me to include your early films in our archives. And Charlie Chaplin …

Louise: Now Oscar, you seem to have come to remind me of my old lovers. This may be an extended visit …

Solbert: (*Pausing briefly.*) I'm sorry, Miss Brooks—uhr, Louise—to make this visit so brief, but I must be going. Another appointment. (*He takes her hand.*) It has been a treat to meet you.

Louise: Oscar, nice of you to stop by. Perhaps we can soon have a longer conversation.

(*Card, smiling, escorts Solbert to back of stage. The audience can hear them whisper.*)

Solbert: James, that is a very strange woman …

Card: Not really, General. When you get to know her you'll learn she is quite exceptional—in many ways. (*Laughing as he returns to sit besides Louise.*) I'd love to hear the general relate this encounter to his wife, who will probably ban him from any future meeting between the two of you.

Louise: I heard that "quite exceptional." Thanks, Jimmy. Lately, I've come to wondering about my being "exceptional." Last week I was listening to Toronto radio and caught a press conference with the actress Ava Gardner. After seeing *The Night of the Iguana*, I didn't think much of her acting and her beauty never excited me ...

Card: Yes ... I was your escort to the theater.

Louise: In the interview, there was nothing about great acting. Yet, for the first time in my life, I was proud to be a movie actress. Ava is in essence what I think a movie star should be: a beautiful person with a unique, mysterious personality unpolluted by Hollywood. She did not have to run away to keep from being turned into a product of the production machine. Why couldn't I have reflected that quality of integrity that makes Ava shine with her own light?

Card: Louise, you have your own style of both strength and integrity.

Louise: So I would like to believe.

Card: Tell me, Louise, why did you leave Hollywood, and where did you go?

Louise: My final movie was a crappy part in a western, and I realized that if this continued what reputation I had earned as an actor would fade. That was in 1938, but I continued rejecting all parts offered. That was a mistake. Sex and booze invited a reputation as a Hollywood whore.
So, in 1940, I departed Hollywood forever and returned to my home in Kansas.

Card: (*Smiling*) California to Kansas! I can't think of a more dissimilar environment.

Louise: You bet it was. But Wichita had become as alien to me as had Hollywood. I opened a dance studio, but the natives avoided me—some because I had once been famous, others because I was considered a failure. So, in 1943, I packed my bags and headed to New York.

Now to my writing. I am about to read but a brief part of my *Remembering Charlie Chaplin*, one who taught me much about acting, who became a very good friend, and—not part of the story-one of my most fun-loving lovers.

Card: (*Smiling*) This, I shall enjoy ...

Louise: You better! But first, how was your visit to Rome?

Card: Great. *The Last Days of Pompeii*. Filmed in 1908 along with the 1912 *Quo Vadis* will soon be in our archives. Anything interesting happen during my absence?

Louise: I've gotten much older ... at least I feel much older.

Card: (*Smiling*) Of course, I've been gone all of three weeks.

Louise: I've been viewing some of my Hollywood films. Jimmy, how the hell did I grow so ugly?

Card: It's all of forty years, Louise. And your life-style, you must admit, played a role.

Louise: Another reminder of my years of unlimited sex and gin?

Card: (*Smiling*) That might have had some effect"...

Louise: I'll buy your verdict as to the impact of gin. But as for sex, there is no such thing as too much. Often, it was only a petulant way to pass the time waiting for another studio to call. Besides, it made me feel young again. Will you grant me that?

Card: That, my dear, is not for me to grant; it was yours to do with as you would.

Louise: (*Laughing*) And you can bet I would. Dammit. *Why* am I not more attractive? (*In a sing-song voice*) Where oh where have my lovers gone?

Card: To change the subject, I read "Gish and Garbo" you wrote for London's *Sight and Sound*. You most certainly are a talented writer.

Louise: Thanks, Jimmy. And I've published many more—feature articles about many more Hollywood characters I knew something about.

Card: Such as ...?

Louise: Humphrey Bogart, an actor that learned on the stage from British actors. And Marlene, Marian Davies, Norma Shearer, Joan Bennet, and Buster Keaton. And what really stimulated me, I wrote about Pabst.

Card: (*Smiling*) Any of your writings rejected?

Louise: You damn right some were rejected, and some that were published have been slammed by critics.

Card: Did that trouble you?

Louise: It sure as hell did. Anyone who thinks criticism and rejection are good for a writer is nuts. You get scarred with rejections. And you may be sure every publisher who turned down your submission robbed you of a little faith in yourself. And what I especially disliked was to be told that what I had written was not "suitable" for publication. SUITABLE! There's been nothing pornographic in what I write. Nor so subversive as to draw the attention of the FBI director, Mr. Hoover. Some, I suppose, might have been controversial enough to scare off magazine publishers who live off studio releases.

(*Telephone rings and Louise answers.*)

Louise: Hello! Yes, John. Are you sure? I had planned on coming to your office. Well, if you feel it is OK to mail the check ... My best wishes to Bill. Bye.

(*Louise hangs up and turns to Card.*)

Louise: That was Bill Paley's assistant, John Minary, who runs the Paley Foundation. I usually pick up my monthly allowance check, but John insists it's quite safe to mail. If it doesn't show up in the mail in the next couple of days, he'll damed well hear from me.

Card: I gather the head of CBS is quite generous ...

Louise: We have remained very good friends, and when l was really desperate for living expenses—back in the early fifties—his private philanthropic foundation in support of the arts provided me a regular monthly allowance to support my writing. And it is to continue indefinitely. It simply reflects Bill Paley's faith in my writing.

(*Retrieves a red file from the table.*) Now, I'll confirm his judgment by reading what I've written about Charlie Chaplin. But first let me tell you about a couple of letters I received. *Playboy* magazine asked me to do an article about sex in the twenties. (*Smiling*) I have no idea as to why they asked me ...

Card: I can guess. And what did you decide?

Louise: I wrote back and said, "Sure, but you can't change a word of what I submit." They would turn it into tits and make-believe sex for their horny readers. They do not give a damn about film history. Of course, I'll never hear back.

Card: That's my Lulu ...

Louise: Lulu was another life ... And I had a letter from a publisher about my autobiography. "Please send your manuscript for us to consider." Consider! If I were to write my autobiography—which I most certainly will not—it will be sent to be published, not considered! Now to what I am willing to write about. I will read but a brief part of my *Remembering Charlie Chaplin*.

Card: (*Smiling*) Finally! I await with keen interest ...

Louise: As I expect. But you'll get but a sample. You'll read the full account when published. I have already decided on the title: *Lulu in Hollywood*.

Card: Fair enough. Have at it.

Louise: (*Opens red file and reads.*) *It was New York, August 1925.*

Chaplin, aged thirty-six, was in town for the premiere of The Gold Rush *at the Strand Theater on*

Broadway. I, aged eighteen, was dancing at the Ziegfeld Follies round the corner at the new Amsterdam Theater on Forty-Second Street. Submerged in my own fascinating being, I was only vaguely aware that The Gold Rush had brought Chaplin his greatest triumph—that he was the toast of all intellectual, cultural, and social New York and that for a week the tabloids ran front-page pictures of Broadway beauties asking "Who bit Charlie's lip?" Then, one afternoon at a cocktail party given by Walter Wanger, I met him.

Don't doze off, Jimmy, I have more to offer ...

Card: I'm wide-awake ... eager to hear more ...

Louise: *His—Chaplin, that is—physical presence revealed an exquisiteness the screen could not reflect. Small, perfectly made, meticulously dressed, with his fine grey hair and ivory skin and white teeth. He was as clean as a pearl and glowed all over. Inside he was glowing too, with the radiant gaiety released by the successful conclusion of two year's work on the film. Taken at this time for Vanity Fair magazine was the Edward Steichen photograph. Chaplin is grinning with infectious naughtiness into the camera at the same time Steichen has caught his horned curls in a faun shadow on the background.*

That, Mr. James Card, is all for now.

Card: (*Silent for a moment*) Louise, when I visited at your apartment in New York, I urged you to come to Rochester and offered to assist you in publishing your experiences. Well, you certainly require no assistance as a writer. You reflect a keen memory and faultless eye for detail. Once again, I urge you to write your autobiography.

Louise: No, Jimmy, that I will not do.

Card: Can I know why you are so reluctant?

Louise: In writing the history of a life, I believe absolutely that the reader cannot understand the character and deeds of the subject unless given a basic understanding of that person's sexual loves and hates and conflicts. It is the only way the reader can make sense out of many apparently senseless actions. It is true that many autobiographies are written to excite, to make money. But in serious books, characters remain as baffling, as unknowable, as ever. Thus, Mr. Card, I too am unwilling to write the sexual truth that would make my life worth reading. I cannot unbuckle my home in Kansas ... in the Bible Belt.

Card: Well put, Louise. (*Smile*) But what you read does seem a bit autobiographical.

Louise: (*Returning the smile.*) Perhaps a bit, Jimmy, but not all.

(*The lights dim, then rise, and the cast and the play-wright take their bow.*)

Playwright: I'm Bob Huddleston, chair of Play-Readers. Thanks for coming, and I thank Jimmy Card and Louise Brooks for their fine performance. (Holding up a copy of *Lulu in Hollywood*.) This copy is earmarked for the Carolina Meadows library, and I have scheduled *Louise Brooks: Looking For Lulu*, a sixty-minute film narrated by actress Shirley MacLaine to be shown in the lecture hall. It includes interviews with Louise Brooks and adds to what you have experienced tonight. Thanks again for coming to PlayReaders.

The Long Snooze

A 25th Anniversary Fantasy

An original play
written as part of Carolina Meadows'
Twenty-Fifth Anniversary celebration.
Performed on December 7, 2010,
featuring Rita Borden, Jim Seitzer,
and Don Stedman with Bill Falconer.

The Characters

R. van Winkle: of the Greatest Generation

Brenda Starstruck: a newspaper reporter

Kevin Stedman: a baby boomer

Dooley Wilson: at the piano

The Play

The play is set in the Carolina Meadows Club Center Lobby. It is a day in October 2010. A man is seated on a chair reading the 2010 *VOICES*, the retirement community's literary journal. The Twenty-Fifth Anniversary banner is projected on the wall. Beside the chair is a small table with a Twenty-Fifth Anniversary coffee mug. A young lady enters and greets the man.

Starstruck: Mr. Winkle, I'm Brenda Starstruck of *Newsworthy News*. (*Winkle starts to rise, but she stops him. They shake hands and she sits.*) As I mentioned over the phone, we're doing a feature about old ... er, senior citizens and how they view the world today. Thanks very much for agreeing to be interviewed.

Winkle: (*Grouchy voice*) Had to skip my yoga class ...

Starstruck: Sorry about that. First off, Mr. Winkle, tell me how you view the situation today—satisfied or otherwise?

Winkle: Headed to hell in a handbasket.

Starstruck: Can you expand on that?

Winkle: Nope

Starstruck: (*A bit flustered.*) Well, sir. How do you feel about the issue of global warming?

Winkle: Hot issue ...

Starstruck: Anything else?

Winkle: Nope

Starstruck: How do you feel about the government in Washington?

Winkle: Get what you deserve.

Starstruck: Let me turn to a very important issue: what is your take on the immigration situation?

Winkle: Keep the food, deport the cooks.

Starstruck: (*Smiling*) You must like Mexican food.

Winkle: Only with cold beer

Starstruck: Might I have your view on the national debt?

Winkle: We're in a deep hole ...

Starstruck: And ... ?

Winkle: Digging deeper

Starstruck: Any suggestion to offer our readers?

Winkle: Spend less than you take in.

Starstruck: You mean higher taxes?

Winkle: Nope.

Starstruck: Might I have your view of the war in Iraq? Do you believe our troops will be out of there by the end of 2011?

Winkle: Nope.

Starstruck: (*Slightly flustered.*) Well ... well ... When do you feel we might be out?

Winkle: Never!

Starstruck: (*Incredulous*) Never? Seriously ... Never?

Winkle: It ends when I die.

Starstruck: Yes, yes, I understand. (*Which, of course, she doesn't.*) But we are making progress, aren't we?

Winkle: Like a hamster on a treadmill.

Starstruck: (*Standing and offering her hand.*) Well, Mr. van Winkle. This has been wonderful. You have provided our readers with much to think about.

Winkle: (*Shaking her hand.*) Computers replaced thinking.

(*Starstruck departs. Winkle sips his coffee, then yawns, and leaves the stage with his VOICES 2010. As he departs, we hear the song "As Time Goes By." A Fiftieth Anniversary banner has replaced the earlier banner projected on the wall. Winkle returns wearing a long beard as the music ends. He sits and soon falls asleep. A younger man enters and notices the old man and goes over and shakes him gently.)*

Stedman: Hey, old timer. Wake up.

Winkle: (*Opening his eyes and shaking his head.*) Huh? What? What'da you want?

Stedman: You sure you're in the right place? This is the Club Center of Carolina Meadows.

Winkle: Of course it is. I live in Pioneer Precinct 7 ... A darn reporter wore me out. I'm waiting for the ceremony. Hey ... you're Don Stedman. You've done a great job organizing the twenty-fifth anniversary celebration ...

Stedman: (*Laughing*) You got that last part right ... but that was my dad, I'm Kevin Stedman, chair of the fiftieth anniversary celebration.

Winkle: Com'on, Don. Stop pulling my leg. I might 'a dozed a bit but not for twenty-five years. (*He sips the coffee.*) Darn, this is cold ...

Stedman: Whatever you say, old fellow. (*Raises his voice.*) Can you hear me, old fellow? It is October 21, 2035, and Carolina Meadow's fiftieth celebration begins today.

Winkle: Stop shouting. I'm trying to get a handle on this ...

Stedman: See that banner on the wall. (*Turns and points to the banner on the wall.*) See that? Fiftieth Anniversary, 1985–2035. (*Shows Winkle his Kindle 200XL.*) Here, read this ... it's a list of events for today. See the date? October 2035. (*He sits besides the old man.*)

Winkle: Well ... I'll be go to hell! Man, I must 'a dozed through a helluva lot.

Stedman: You sure did. What did you say your name was? And speak louder—like all Boomers, I'm a bit deaf.

Winkle: (*Loudly*) R. van Winkle. They call me "Van." Deaf, you say. Figures ... hard rock music .. .l saw it coming ...

Stedman: Well, van, you must have nodded off in October 2010. And things sure have changed. (*Laughs*) For one thing, we Baby Boomers have taken over.

Winkle: Well, if it really is 2035, I guess my generation has moved on ...

Stedman: You bet. Our last survey showed, you know, almost 100 percent of Baby Boomers living in independent living. The last of what you guys called the Greatest Generation was an old duffer named Joe Mengel. They say he was 105—plus or minus a few years. And when they dragged him out of his villa, he was clutching his favorite putter.

Winkle: That's the Joe Mengel I remember. Great guy with a wedge. Tell me, Don—I mean "Kevin"—has Carolina Meadows gotten many Baby Boomers from across the road, Governors Club?

Stedman: Yes, they favor Carolina Meadows over the Cedars.

Winkle: They can be good neighbors—except when a Duke fan sneaks in ...

Stedman: Glad to know you're a UNC supporter.

Winkle: You betcha—ever since my dad took me to my first game. I saw Choo Choo run rings around the Duke defenders. 'Course, you know about Choo Choo ...

Stedman: Sounds like a chewing gum ...

Winkle: Don't you be disrespectful, young man. Charlie "Choo Choo" Justice was the Tar Heels' greatest running back. ... How about lately? Any players who can play football like Choo Choo?

Stedman: Sorry to have to tell you this, old fellow: no more football—not at UNC, not at Duke. Football as you know it is out in America.

Winkle: What!

Stedman: Football ended when the Supreme Court ruled that the teams had to diversify...

Winkle: You mean more white players?

Stedman: Women ... half the players had to be women. The Supreme Court ruled that separate was not equal.

Winkle: OK. So now we sock it to Duke in basketball. ..

Stedman: Nope ... basketball is out with football. Even before the Title IX decision, basketball was endangered because of a suit by the League of Average-Sized Americans ...

Winkle: The WHAT?

Stedman: LASA—League of Average Size Americans. They won a lower court decision that ruled that 50 percent of basketball players had to be under six feet.

Winkle: What's left? Can we whack the Dukies in soccer and baseball?

Stedman: Nope, soccer and baseball went the way of football.

Winkle: What's with the high schools? Square dancing?

Stedman: No, the Supreme Court ruled that young people, seventeen and under, were excepted. The reasoning was that their height and sexual orientation had not yet fully formed.

Winkle: Hooray! I'd apply that reasoning to Baby Boomers.

Stedman: I'll ignore that.

Winkle: Well, you young people have sure turned life upside down. I expect you'll be telling me we have to beat Duke in bocce ...

Stedman: Sorry, no way. Duke keeps fielding great bocce players.

Winkle: Well, goody, goody. There must be some sport left ...

Stedman: There is ... bocce is a minor competitive sport. The big one now is cricket.

Winkle: Cricket! Young fella, you've got to find me some sleeping pills. I can't take this! Football out. Basketball, baseball, and soccer, no more. And now you're telling me we've got to take Duke on in cricket, the game played by English pussycats.

Stedman: Actually, it was the Indian students that introduced the game. But some changes were introduced. American players, men and women, wear white shorts rather than long trousers, but the women's shorts are a bit shorter. No challenge in the courts as yet.

Winkle: And both sexes pause, no doubt, for tea and crumpets.

Stedman: You sure can be snarly when you wake up, old timer.

Winkle: Heck, son. I'm snarly all the time, but you've raised it to a new height. Let's get off the subject of the decline and fall of sports. How about bringing me up to date on other happenings.

Stedman: Well, when you walk around the campus, you know, change will smack you in the face ...

Winkle: I mean, how about the outside world. When I dozed off, Barack Obama was president. How'd he make out?

Stedman: From what is taught in school, all things considered, he was a pretty good president, not as good as Harry Truman, but a cut above Eisenhower. He won a second term, then became president of the University of Chicago. His wife, Michelle, is on the US Supreme Court ...

Winkle: Wow! The Supreme Court! That is interesting ...

Stedman: Let me add that since President Obama, we have not elected a white, Anglo-Saxon, Protestant male president. (*Laughs*) We just ain't got the voting power we once had. The Supreme

Court is now six women and three males—and I suspect one is gay.

(*Pause.*)

Winkle: Now I understand what has happened to sports.

Stedman: The decision was unanimous.

Winkle: How about the wars in Afghanistan and Iraq?

Stedman: We still have troops in Afghanistan, but we're making progress with the end in sight. Just last week, Madam President announced that the tide had turned. The 2034 spring offensive was successful, and the war should end by the end of this year.

Winkle: By the end of 2035? The president said the end of 2011 before I dozed off ...

Stedman: Be patient, old fellow. We got out of Iraq about ten years ago, but the Sunnis and Shiites still can't get along. Many so-called Wise Leaders say they never will. Stateside, however, there is much you'll appreciate ...

Winkle: I'm all ears ...

Stedman: All major cities are now connected by high-speed rail. French built, of course. And no gas or diesel vehicles are allowed on interstate highways ...

Winkle: Great. Long overdue. And I hope the trains serve French cuisine.

Stedman: Nope. Mexican food is featured. But the train reaches 250 mph between Charlotte and Wilmington—and no crossings.

Winkle: Well, I certainly hand it to you Baby Boomers—nothing better than Mexican food with cold beer.

Stedman: There is a down side ... We had to pay the French for the trains, Mexico to prepare the rail lines, India to provide engineers. And, of course, all paid with borrowed money ...

Winkle: I should have guessed ... from China, no doubt.

Stedman: Yeah, and about ten years ago they decided to call in some of the debt.

Winkle: Wow! I bet Washington panicked ...

Stedman: You could hear the howling all the way to Chicago. Treasury sought to restructure the loans, but the Chinese drove a hard bargain.

Winkle: Such as ...

Stedman: A ninety-nine-year lease on the Grand Canyon.

(*Pause.*)

Winkle: You're not serious!

Stedman: The Chinese were dead serious. They saw it as a real money-maker—millions of Chinese tourists. And our negotiators were of a mind to go along until the states bordering on the canyon ganged-up to force it off the table ...

Winkle: What then?

Stedman: The Chinese came back with "take it or else we'll call in all loans." We folded ...

Winkle: And we gave ... ?

Stedman: Alaska—lock, stock, and all the oil. With the moose a sweetener. And would you believe—it drew popular support.

Winkle: That surprises me.

Stedman: Probably because Sarah Palin—you must remember her—had retired to her home town of Wasilla and refused to budge.

(*Pause.*)

Winkle: Well, we did get Alaska cheap (*laughing*) ... and no capital gains to pay. Seriously, this must'a created a serious problem.

Stedman: How's that?

Winkle: All American flags would have had to be replaced with 49 stars ...

Stedman: Easily solved. Congress, then controlled by the Tea Party, saw a chance to save money ...

Winkle: They abolished the American flag?

Stedman: Of course not. In order to keep the flag with fifty stars, they voted Puerto Rico into the Union.

Winkle: (*Sarcastically*) Great ... an all-Hispanic state.

Stedman: True. And their campaign to make Spanish our official language is gaining traction.

Winkle: I've heard enough of the Outside World. I've a mind to go back to sleep. But before I do, tell me, what have you Baby Boomers done to Carolina Meadows?

Stedman: (*Laughing*) Well, for one thing, the golf course is long gone.

Winkle: You must be joking ...

Stedman: Nope. We Baby Boomers put pressure on, you know, to convert the land to organic farming. Golf was proven to cause serious mental problems. Besides, too many overworked joints had to be replaced.

Winkle: This is hard to digest ...

Stedman: Well, you can, you know, digest wonderful organic vegetables. The first fairway is devoted to broccoli, the second to tomatoes, the third to arugula. I've forgotten where kale and turnips are grown ...

Winkle: Spare me ...

Stedman: Not the entire nine holes. The sixth fairway provides us with free-range chickens and the ninth with fresh goat's milk.

Winkle: I'll bet you will be telling me that the old fenced-in garden patch is now a pig pen.

Stedman: Heavens no! That is now devoted to growing marijuana ...

Winkle: Now I know you're joking ...

Stedman: Not at all. Before I moved in—it was 2013 or 14—a federal law permitted residents of continuing care retirement communities unlimited use of marijuana, provided it was actually grown on their property and smoked only by residents.

Winkle: Well, at least not all changes have been bad. Now about this organic vegetable business. I bet our great chef, Mark Maxwell, created some wonderful dishes.

Stedman: I know him only by reputation ... he had gone before I moved in ...

Winkle: Retired?

Stedman: No, I understand he was lured away by that retirement place up the road we call Park Avenue West. Also called The Cedars ...

Winkle: I'd have bet big money against that. He loved Carolina Meadows, and we loved him.

Stedman: Well, van, Old timers say the food got so bad at Park Avenue West that a mutiny was building up among the resident plutocrats ... The owners came to Maxwell and offered him 10 percent ownership.

Winkle: That sounds like big bucks ...

Stedman: Not enough—he laughed and, to shut 'em up, said it would take more like 50 percent.

Winkle: So?

Stedman: (*Laughing*) It's been said they gave him 50 percent and control of the whole shebang—not just dining.

Winkle: Man! That would be big bucks!

Stedman: Real big bucks. In five years he had the place as good as Carolina Meadows, sold his interest, and went into business for himself ...

Winkle: I'm all ears ...

Stedman: Remember the John Edwards estate?

Winkle: All the talk back then ...

Stedman: Well, Maxwell bought it and established the Maxwell Culinary Institute ...

Winkle: And, I'll bet, darn successful.

Stedman: World renowned ... students from France fight to get in. It has practically put that New York CIA out of business. It's still tops, though Maxwell retired from active involvement about ten years ago ...

Winkle: Good for him.

Stedman: It's legend here that shortly following his move into the Edwards estate, Mark showed up at our front door in a yellow Rolls-Royce Phantom. He stopped briefly at the Club Center to visit with our chef, then said he was going for a nostalgic tour of the campus. Word spread, and old-timers rushed out to wave as he passed ...

Winkle: Of course ... He was loved by all. Besides, one doesn't see a yellow Rolls-Royce every day.

Stedman: It wasn't just the Rolls and Mark, the chauffeur was none other than Jody Hite, our activities director, who had retired a few years earlier.

Winkle: Jody, our Master Multitasker! She who could bounce many balls in the air and drop nary a one. I wish someone had wakened me to join the cheering!

Stedman: Yeah, and I wish I'd been there. By the way, when Jody retired, it was estimated that she had shuffled over 10,000 chairs in the auditorium during her years at Carolina Meadows.

Winkle: Musta been at least 10,000 before I dozed off. Back to John Edwards. What happened to him ... and his girlfriend, Hunter... Rielle Hunter?

Stedman: Oh, he and Rielle have the penthouse in Building 12 ...

Winkle: Penthouse!

Stedman: Well, with the population growth and limited land to expand, we had to go up. All new apartment buildings have twelve floors.

Winkle: How have you dealt with dining?

Stedman: Down! We have a great Rathskeller, draft beer, and local venison is the specialty.

Winkle: Does that handle a larger number for dining?

Stedman: Not at all. On Buildings 9 and 10 we have roof gardens—the favorite places for Sunday brunch. By the way, the one on Building 10 is favored by the residents from Fearrington who love the beltedburgers ...

Winkle: The what?

Stedman: The chef named it the beltedburgers ... Made from belted cows ... great! But speaking of food, you must be darn hungry. The roof garden on Building 10 isn't open, so how about a Big Mac?

Winkle: (*Incredulous*) A WHAT? A Big Mac?

Stedman: (*Laughing*) You heard correctly … a Big Mac. Carolina Meadows had a liquidity problem, so we decided to sell the cafe to McDonalds.

Winkle: But … but … Big Macs don't go with organic vegetables …

Stedman: Listen, old timer, my generation holds on to certain traditions—Big Macs along with Krispy Kreme donuts, Hard Rock and Levis as formal dress are all carved in stone. But your generation held to the tradition of cheap gas, polluted air, and polluted water …

Winkle: Point made, but Big Macs and Krispy Kreme donuts will do you in …

Stedman: Not as fast as dirty water and dirty air did yours.

Winkle: Well, your diet does take some pressure off Social Security and Medicare …

Stedman: How's that?

Winkle: Never mind. Something else, young fellow. Your daddy created a time capsule during the twenty-fifth anniversary, to be opened this year. I want to see the look on you youngsters when you open it.

Stedman: Interesting you should bring that up, old fellow. We opened the time capsule last night.

Winkle: Last night! You told me the fiftieth celebration started today.

Stedman: We had to jump the gun to please the local TV station, Fox News, the only news outlet in the state. They had a program, and they wanted it included ...

Winkle: OK, so whadda you think about Carolina Meadows twenty-five years ago? Pretty interesting place, wasn't it?

Stedman: Big surprise. Dad told me what to expect, but it wasn't what we found when we opened the capsule ...

Winkle: What do you mean?

Stedman: Someone—probably in the dead of night—opened the box and replaced the entire contents.

Winkle: With what?

Stedman: A book, and one with a silly title—*Arguing with Idiots* by a guy named Glen Beck. He hasn't been around in years, but I've read he was a popular TV commentator in his day ...

Winkle: Yeah, he was. To some people, but not here at Carolina Meadows. Any clue as to who pulled off the caper?

Stedman: It came with a note: "Compliments of the Triangle Tea Party, October 12, 2012." That's all we know, so far.

Winkle: Well, it was a Nixon-type dirty trick. Did anyone think to check for prints?

Stedman: That we did. One of our residents is a former federal agent. He lifted two sets and had a friend run them through the national database ...

Winkle: And?

Stedman: One set was dad's, of course. The second was a resident named Jack Parry. Remember him?

Winkle: Parry? Sure. He loved practical jokes—known as Joker Jack. But the Parry I knew would accept being waterboarded before he'd have anything to do with the Beck character. Besides, he was a key player in creating the time capsule, which would explain the prints.

Stedman: Then the mystery will go unsolved.

Winkle: Too bad! Hey, let's go eat one of your Big Macs or a beltedburger and die young. Well, one of us will die young. Later, drop me off in the library ... I'll pick up some books I've missed ...

Stedman: Sorry, old fellow ... we don't have books or newspapers or tapes or compact discs. We all read and get our entertainment electronically— all those old dust-covered books and stuff are long gone ...

Winkle: No library ... sad

Stedman: But put to good use! We leased the room to Starbucks ... Most residents stay home, but some bring their Kindles, laptops, or iPods and have a cappuccino. Some even prefer to relax with a joint. Here, van, let me give you a hand ...

(Stedman helps Winkle up. As they leave the stage, Winkle shakes his head.)

Winkle: I hope to hell when I wake up, the damn beard is gone and I forget this godawlful future.

Stedman: What are you muttering about, old fella?

(As they leave the stage, the audience applauds. The three characters return to take their bows. The play-wright joins them and announces that refreshments are in the back of the auditorium. The piano player plays "As Time Goes By.")

ROBERT HUDDLESTON was awarded the coveted silver wings of an Army Air Corps pilot while still a teenager. This was followed by extensive training in the P-47 Thunderbolt fighter, the aircraft he would pilot in combat against German military forces in the air and on the ground in World War II.

After the war, a university education under the GI Bill was followed by employment at New Mexico's White Sands Missile Range, where German rocket experts were employed. He then moved onto Washington, DC, to work at the Pentagon before joining the newly established space agency NASA, first at the Goddard Space Flight Center in nearby Maryland, later at NASA headquarters. Huddleston has degrees from the University of Missouri and George Washington University, and he graduated from the

National Defense University in Washington, DC, as a representative of NASA.

He married Pepita Lassalle on September 18, 1974. Departing federal service, he became a freelance writer publishing articles, essays, book reviews, and short stories. For ten years, he was a columnist for the *Federal Times*. He has also published a biography of his wife's father, a Mexican-American patriot, *Edmundo: From Chiapas, Mexico, to Park Avenue* (2007); the novella *An American Pilot with the Luftwaffe* (2014); the novel *Love and War: A Father and Son in Two World Wars* (2020); *Satan's Henchman: Whatever Became of SS General Hans Kammler?* (2023), a work of historical fiction; and *A Most Remarkable Life: The Collected Works of Bob Huddleston, Volume 1* (2023). Now a widower, he resides in a retirement community in Chapel Hill, North Carolina. The fact that he is fast approaching his 100th birthday in 2024 has in no way slowed down his writing.